Of
Trains

and
Other
Things

Jeff Howe

www.thejeffhowe.com

© 2008 by Jeff Howe

First printing.

ISBN: 1438242735

Printed in the United States

Table of Contents

FOREWORD

Jeff Howe is a storyteller. He doesn't fib, and there is no malice but nevertheless he does tell stories.

Now in his late forties, he has refined these stories to magnetic qualities. They draw the reader in and grip him by the throat forcing him to gag to find out more and often leaving him hanging perilously over a wilderness lurch. I have not read a collection since I was drawn to Isaac Asimov as a teenager .

Not one of the following stories is true. There are Uncle Leos out there and maybe some of them sensed an extraordinary smell. But they won't be this Uncle Leo. This is a compilation of the strange, the mystical, the spiritual and the ghostly. It will make you laugh and make you wonder. It will also make you think about similar situations you have yourself encountered, and it will make you think of them in a new light. This is the power of the story teller.

I first found Jeff on a poetry website where his eloquence lifted him above his peers. As a short story writer he has now upset a whole new peer group.

Rols Sperling
Publisher, Writer
www.madjockpublishers.com

INTRODUCTION
On Writing

The creative process for me, is not a comfortable process. I like having ideas, and I like having an end product that fulfills my vision for it. It's all the steps in between that cause me to grit my teeth, curse at the medium and make me feel like putting my fist through a wall. It doesn't matter if I'm writing stories, songs, poetry or painting a picture. The process is all the same to me.

I wonder at people who can get up in the morning and write 100,000 words before lunch. I really do. Just scratching out 1000 words over the course of a day can be incredibly agonizing. I think it's because I seek *alla prima* perfection. I want to get it right and good and jaw-dropping the first time through. Or at least I used to.

Now I just want to get it good. I want to get it finished.

I used to think that I could never write a story because I never seemed to have any ideas. You have to know what you are going to write about before you write it, right? Surely, Stephen King knew exactly how *The Mist* was going to be mapped out before he even typed the first word. Kurt Vonnegut had to have written *Welcome to the Monkey House* from copious notes he'd made prior to starting. What about O. Henry's *The Gift of the Magi*? Definitely outlined, 1st drafted, 2nd drafted and edited and final drafted.

I imagine what I'm saying is true, though it's really speculation on my part. Some people seem born to story-telling while others need to have it squeezed out of them.

Most of my stories have started with just a concept. Then as I start writing, more and more of the narrative reveals itself to me until I end up with a story. I don't usually get stuck for long periods of time wondering what comes next, but there are definite slow downs in the race of imagination. On the other hand, some sections zip by quite quickly. I love those sections. They feel like the old brain is firing cleanly on all cylinders, that the language is easy and flowing. They are the times when it seems like I am fully engaged in the process and not merely trying to get through it.

Here's how each of the stories happened.

The Concourse was the result of a dream I had one night. The only thing about the dream I remember is being in a subway concourse and hearing a horrible noise emanating up from a lower level.

The Train is the result of wanting to write a story where the character rides on a subway train and ends up in a place that is quite unfamiliar, perhaps even strange. I remember something similar when I exited the Lechmere station on Boston's MBTA.

The Forest in Forever came through a desire to write something that captured a feeling similar to what I experience when I read Stephen King's short stories, *The Reach* and *Mrs. Todd's Shortcut.*

The Box was a way for me to catharsize (if there's such a word) the death of my wife's father, the first of the parent-level deaths in our family.

Waiting for Sherrie was inspired by finding the site of an old girlfriend on classmates.com. However, I haven't tried to contact her like Mark does.

The Tracks simply started out with the words, "Spring is a woman." I had written the beginning portion of it long before I actually finished the story. I had no idea what to do with it until I came up with the idea of a trilogy of train stories. Then the mental video reel started running.

Overheard at the Game was a desire to capture some of the dynamics of a Little League baseball game in a small town from the standpoint of the spectators. A couple of the conversations were based on actual ones I heard at different games.

A Brave New World was inspired by a YouTube video of a teen playing the video game Guitar Hero. After I saw the video, I read the comments left by others who had seen it.

The Six O'Clock News just happened. The only impetus I can remember is that I wrote it for a correspondence course my wife was taking. She couldn't come up with an idea, so I did it for her.

Uncle Leo's Nose was an idea I had about a gentleman who could smell things other people couldn't.

With the exception of **Overheard at the Game**, the stories originated with only a seed of an idea. When I started writing, the seed germinated and eventually grew into the finished product. I've had to rewrite portions of some of the stories when they started growing in directions I didn't like. But that usually comes after the body of the work has been finished and fine tuning becomes the task.

So that's pretty much how it works for me. I've found that the actual exercise of writing is what brings on the ideas, the story development. Often I have no real clear idea of where a story is going until I'm in the middle of it. Something a character says or does, seemingly out of the blue, will make me say, "Now why did he/she say/do that?" Then I'm left to determine what it means and how it affects the plot. I have read that Dean Koontz writes in a similar fashion.

The process is all very interesting in its way. Sometimes it's amusing as well. But it still remains an exercise in agony for the most part.

Join me in my journeys through the writing process. They are painstakingly created, lovingly shaped and tweaked to the nth degree.

I hope they are good as well.

THE CONCOURSE
(1997)

"Take it easy, Joe," I said, preparing to leave the parking garage booth where I worked. "Catch you tomorrow same time. Oh, by the way, Edna's back. I found her this afternoon on the third level. She was checking out a Silver Shadow Rolls."

Edna is a bag lady who hangs around the garage for a couple of weeks and then disappears for a while. We can usually expect her back around the first of the month. She's a sweet lady in her late fifties, a little bedraggled, somewhat gamey. I once asked her where she went when she wasn't here. She said that she stays with friends.

The management doesn't particularly like Edna hanging around the expensive cars in the garage, so we hide her in a utility closet when they're around; doing whatever it is that management does. We also let her sleep in the utility closet when the weather gets cold. It's heated and roomy enough for her to get quite comfortable. When it's warm - this September has been quite warm - Edna likes to sleep on the upper level of the garage. She calls it her penthouse suite. I try to bring her some soup or a sandwich regularly from a local deli. If I forget, or can't afford it at that time, Edna jokes about how lousy room service is.

Joe, a tall, slender black man, early 20s, grinned and said, "Good. My old lady cooked me somethin' nasty for lunch. I'll give it to Edna and grab somethin' from next door. Have a good night, man."

"Yeah, you too," I replied.

I left the garage and walked down the street toward the subway station. It was 7:00, the third hour in what is ridiculously known as the "rush hour". The passageways of the city were jammed with people who all had one goal - to get home, flip on the tube, and fall asleep on the couch.

I had no plans for the evening; I rarely do, so I strolled easily down the middle of the sidewalk, forcing the crowd to rush around me. I live alone in a small suburban apartment twenty miles south of the city. I had graduated from college over five years ago with a B.A. in Psychology, a wonderful preparation for collecting money in a parking garage. But the economy is slow - jobs are scarce. I felt fortunate to get a cheap rent which allowed me the luxury of not having to have a roommate.

I paused before entering the gaping maw that rose above the sidewalk and led down to the subway station concourse. The tall monuments of glass and stone which towered above me poked the rosy purple clouds with their spindly fingers. Rivulets of people swirled and eddied through the canyons created by the monuments. I smiled at the warmth of the deeply westering sun as its rich golden aura cast the city into a mythical dimension that rivaled the realm of Olympus. Closing my eyes, I inhaled the sweet, clean evening breeze tinged with luscious fragrances from the nearby Italian restaurants as they prepared for their dinner trade. Then I turned to descend the stairwell into the concourse.

On the first step I stopped for a moment. Like a deja vu, a strong sense of destiny washed over me. It left me a little light-headed. I was unnerved by the feeling. For the past several weeks I'd had a vague feeling that something was ahead of me, lurking just beyond the hazy vapors where my sight began to fade. I don't believe in ESP, predicting the future, or bending spoons with your mind. But I do think that somewhere deep down inside we all have some sort of a miniature radar dish that sends us signals from time to time. The sensation faded quickly, however, so I continued on.

After a couple of steps I could feel the hot fetid breath of the subway station swelling up through the stairwell. A couple more steps and the stale, faintly sour odors that permeate the atmosphere washed over me. My feet sensed a slight shudder coursing through the stairs as I heard the distant rumbling of trains coursing through the caverns below.

The stairwell began regurgitating a torrent of people up toward me. The expressions on their faces and in their eyes reminded me of a term that was born in the Vietnam War; a term that described the distant, vacant look of the battle-weary soldiers. It was the thousand-yard stare. Each person climbing up from the bowels of the city looked blankly through me to the gently darkening skies beyond. I leaned closer to the wall and let the mass flow past me. Soon the crowd thinned leaving only breathless stragglers to weakly heave their way out of the subway exit opening. I reached the bottom of the stairs and fumbled in my pocket for change.

Walking up to the booth, I requested, "One token please."

The man behind the thick glass looked at me indifferently. A hand slid through the slot, curled around the coins I had set on the counter. Then, with a quick flick, it and the money disappeared. In their place, a dull brass subway token remained. The rheumy-eyed face behind the glass continued to stare as if no transaction had ever taken place. I felt like cheering this marvelous display of sleight-of-hand but knew no one would understand the joke.

I turned to the turnstile. Placing the token in the slot, I leaned into the protruding arms. The turning mechanism clicked slowly at first. Then it picked up speed as I brought my weight to bear on the resisting bars. With a sudden ripping sound I was expelled to the other side of the turnstile. I looked back at the row of silent chrome guardians of the station. Somehow I felt as if I had passed a test, or initiation, of sorts.

I was now in the concourse. It was a long, wide corridor leading to the train platforms. My train was bound to be late; there was no big hurry anyway. So I decided to sit on a bench in the concourse for a while instead of going straight to the platform. In the entire subway network, this is probably the most interesting place to watch people. Most subway stations sit on a single line in the system. But this is a multi-level station which means that several different lines in the system converge here. All the lines are named after colors, which, I guess, makes them easily identifiable to illiterate subway riders. At this particular station there are three colors, two primary and one secondary.

First, there is the Blue Line.

Its platforms are further down the corridor and on the left. This line services the airport, so a lot of travelers and business commuters rush through here.

Next there is the Orange Line.

It runs through a lower level. The Orange Line services Chinatown and low income suburbs to the north and south. They are commonly referred to as bad neighborhoods. Its southern terminus is near a large arboretum.

The last is the Red Line.

It is on the upper level. Its tracks emerge into the relatively fresh air of the city above. Several colleges and Irish Catholic communities lie along various points of the Red Line.

In addition to the trains, two giant department stores have basement entrances from the concourse. There are also small businesses - a newsstand, a shoe shine booth, and a donut/coffee concession - lined up along the subterranean walls.

Near one of the department store entrances stood an unkempt man, probably in his late twenties. He was playing a guitar and singing Bob Dylan's "Blowing in the Wind." His guitar case was at his feet. It was wide open to catch whatever change passersby would toss to show appreciation for his music. It seems like a pitiful way to make money, but street musicians are a different breed. A particularly good evening can net the performer a few hundred dollars in change. I heard a college student once brag that he was able to pay about half his tuition just by playing Park Street Station a couple afternoons a week during rush hour. I had once considered giving poetry readings in the subway but decided that would lump me into the same category as street preachers. They don't make any money, and people give them a wide berth.

I sat on a discolored concrete bench and leaned back against the dirty tile wall. The singer was about halfway through the last chorus when I gazed toward him. For a quick, timeless moment I had the impression that he was staring intensely straight into my eyes. A chill ran down my spine. The final words, "blowing in the wind", echoed emptily through the concourse as all other sound and movement seemed to freeze into an amber moment. I thought I saw a faint grin appear on the singer's face. Then the spell was broken. Commuters hurried by. Trains rumbled about.

And the singer was singing "Homeward Bound."

I shivered, wondered if I was going mad. The vague feeling of destiny ad solidified into one big ice cube that tap danced down my back. I ran my hand through my hair, took a deep breath and forced myself to watch the people passing by.

While living in the city I had learned that one does not watch people by staring wide-eyed at each individual as they walk by. Instead, you lean back against the wall, close your eyes halfway, and maintain an expression of utter apathy on your face. This way you can observe while subtly moving your eyes. No one will know, or care, that they re being watched. It's one of the little games that you learn to play when you spend every day among hundreds of people wrapped up in their own worlds. Not everyone plays this way, but I have found hat I can keep up a good shield against any eye-to-eye contact whatsoever. It is a form of camouflage that makes my presence essentially invisible to those nearby, while keeping my senses at full alert to the circumstances around me.

You see a lot of people doing the same thing while wearing sunglasses, but that's too obvious. It takes a real expert to pull it off without them. Of course, there are people who simply don't care if they are caught staring.

I scanned the wide corridor. The activity, which until now had been fairly light, was building up to white-foam frenzy as trains on two levels had just spewed their contents onto the platform. Then they gorged themselves on the waiting commuters, slowly groaned away from the stop and repeated the bulimic procedure at the next station further down the line.

I watched the rhythm, the ballet of the unlikely, as disparate crowds of people made their way up the corridor with the hopes of gasping the fresher air on the surface.

The Pinstripe Suits and Briefcases travel in small groups, usually no larger than three. Their motion is precise, direct and practiced. They always walk through the station with an air of profound purpose, as if their goal is very clear and apparent. Their hard leather heels click sharply: an obbligato to their rigid movement. Their language is obtuse, secretive; it is peppered with words and phrases like "arbitrage" and "leveraged buyout."

The Zippered Leather Jackets and Untied Hightops shamble along with great boisterousness and cacophony. Their voices vie with one another in competition for attention until they echo crazily up and down the tiled corridors. You can hear them long after they've passed. Disjointed gesticulations punctuate every point; their speech becomes machine gun fire. Their laughter, colored with shades of primal aggression, is anathema to the quiet and fearful.

The Blue Jeans and Book Bags usually move unobtrusively in pairs or solo. They are often found browsing at the newsstand and the coffee concession, poring over the latest weekly news or sports magazine with a stale glazed doughnut in one hand and a knapsack hanging on a shoulder. They move through the subway station with mild caution still wearing tatters of fresh curiosity. But each year, as they return to the area to continue their education, those tatters are dissolved by the acidic sights in the bowels of the city until all that remains are walking shadows of childhood. Thus is knowledge born.

While this well-choreographed extravaganza continued to unfold, a bum approached me and rasped, "Got any change you can spare?"

I really dislike being approached in the city. It is always by people who want something from you. My heart beat a little faster. I looked up at him. He had about six day's growth of beard surrounding a mouth that was randomly adorned with brownish yellow teeth. His eyes were spider webs of bright red veins. Though the air in the concourse was close to stifling he was wearing several layers of dirty woolen clothing topped with a knee-length herringbone tweed overcoat. The stench emanating from this man was very similar to that which laced the atmosphere in the station. A silly picture of him hanging in a plastic air freshener wrapper from a cigarette lighter knob in a Buick flickered through my mind.

Then I noticed his fingernails.

At the ends of the dirtiest and most gnarled hands I've ever seen were clean and evenly trimmed fingernails. The contrast surprised me. It made me forget my distaste for being panhandled.

The homily "Give a man a fish and he'll eat for a day, teach a man to fish and he'll eat for life" flitted ridiculously through my mind. My guess is that the person who penned that nice phrase had never spent much time in a subway station.

I stared at the man for a second, then said, "Oh hell, I'm no teacher."

I flipped him the few coins I had in my pocket. He shuffled off muttering his thanks and other words I couldn't quite hear. I watched him for a few minutes, sighed and continued my observations.

By this time Simon and Garfunkel had finished "Homeward Bound" and been replaced with Paul McCartney's "Maybe I'm Amazed."

Another train pulled into the station with a clamor and released its contents. And another. All the while people were passing back and forth, forth and back. I could hear the ripping sound of the turnstiles, now coming across constantly. I could see in many people's eyes a sense of urgency to keep moving. They looked like swimmers almost out of air, struggling for the surface, for the life-giving oxygen above. I understood how they felt. You can become claustrophobic in a subway station especially when you consider the millions of tons of metal, concrete, and humanity that are poised to come crashing down around your head if the supports weaken.

Or maybe they're just in a hurry.

I always considered the hurry-up mentality as kind of strange. Most people aren't really going anywhere of any great consequence, so I can't understand why they would want to get there sooner. But they have attached such an importance to destination that any intermediate phase is viewed as distasteful, though necessary.

My friends tell me that I think too much.

Paul McCartney finished his piece with a flourish. He stepped back, bowed his head. Robbie Robertson stepped forward with "The Weight."

The air seemed to be growing warmer, stuffier. The sense of impending future still sat oppressively on me like a heavy wool blanket. I felt my forehead become slick with perspiration. A sharp desire to be aboveground where the evening air was balmy and comfortable suddenly scourged through me. I looked

9

at my watch. I had already missed two trains. The next wasn't due for another twenty minutes or so. I decided to wait about fifteen minutes, and then I would go on up to the Red Line platform.

The babbling confusion of the concourse remained at its high chaotic level. A man dressed in an expensive suit, obviously impatient and trying to quickly circumvent the slower, denser crowd that plodded through the center of the station, whisked by and stepped on my foot. This caused him to stumble. He shot a nasty glance back at me. When he made an unwholesome comment about my matriarchal lineage, I slowly turned my head toward him and glared directly into his eyes. He was a young pup, rather short and skinny. He had the brash look of a recent Harvard Business School grad.

In a low, even voice I said, "Wha'd you say?"

It may have been my larger build or the fact that my hair is somewhat long and I sport a beard. Or it may have been that I was wearing my old Army camouflage pants and work boots. Or it even could have been the fact that I started to lean forward as if to get up. But the guy's face turned a whiter shade of pale.

He quickly shouted out, "Nothing, sorry!" With that he took off at a dead run.

I slouched back against the wall and let out a short laugh. The intimidation game can be as much fun as the bored-and-seen-it-all game. I don't do it too often, though; it can backfire on you. I remember one time I tried it on a particularly annoying person in a movie theater. He was making a lot of noise which bothered several people around him, including me. I informed him he would have a healthier future if he either shut up or left. He responded by threatening to hand me my testicles on a silver platter. A few minutes later, an usher came by and escorted him out of the building accompanied by applause from the people in that section. As we left the theater after the movie, I saw him leaning up against a nearby building cleaning his fingernails with a large knife.

I'm no fool, and I'm usually not armed. So I turned sharply, slipped back into the crowd slowly moving out of the lobby to find another exit. I don't know if that guy was waiting for me, but there's one thing I've learned about survival in the city. Always be prepared for the worst. And be intelligent enough not to take chances whenever possible.

By this time, the singer had finished "The Weight." He was taking a few moments to tune his guitar. He let out some dissonant twangs which blended nicely, I thought, with the din of the station.

In addition to the commotion caused by the commuters, I could hear the Orange Line rains squealing and grinding on the level below. The stark sounds of metal on metal shrieked through the air and seemed to grow louder. If you've never heard a train struggling through a sharp turn, then you really don't know audio agony. The wheels, which are semi-fixed in a forward direction, actually fight the curved track, so the train has to move slowly or it will derail. The resulting sound is like a cross between a cat fight and the scraping of fingernails over a blackboard.

It was starting to get uncomfortably hot. I could feel little drops of sweat running down my back. My shirt was sticking to me. I knew that part of the rise in temperature was due to the hundreds of bodies passing through the station. But even so, it was as if someone had turned on the large heating blowers that hung from the ceiling. My back began to ache from the uncomfortable bench, so I decided it was time to leave.

The crowd, by now, was beginning to thin down to a few stragglers. I heard the rattling of metal as the underground concessions pulled the protective doors over their facades. The business end of the concourse as winding down. I knew that the commuters from this point on would mostly be theatergoers, barhoppers, and nightlifers, with the occasional research library-bound student.

I stood, stretched and headed for the Red Line platform. A feeling of relief spread through me with the anticipation of leaving this tomb. But, underneath, the restless, nagging feeling wouldn't die.

I reached the stairs leading up to the platform and started climbing. Sweat was now rolling down my forehead, stinging my eyes. The stairwell seemed longer and steeper than I remembered. I was panting from the exertion.

Then I heard my train roll into the station above.

Scared that I would miss it, I climbed as fast as I could. With heart racing and muscles screaming, I finally reached the top of the stairwell. As I stepped onto the platform, I felt the clean, cool air of the night brush over my damp body. It refreshed me and lifted my spirits, filling me with an unexpected joy. I released a long breath of relief and knew now, more than ever, that I just wanted to go home.

The train sat waiting patiently on the tracks with its doors wide open. It gleamed in the pale moonlight like a bright silver bullet. There seemed to be a deep blue aura surrounding the cars. The scene was quiet and peaceful. One by one, stars twinkled in the black velvet sky. I walked up to the turnstile and reached into my pocket.

A feeling of horror crept over me as I realized that I had only bought one token. The horror was quickly replaced by confusion as I remembered that this platform never had turnstiles before. Before I could figure out what was going on, I heard the doors gently close with a sigh. I looked at the train.

The driver was standing in his compartment gazing out his window at me. He smiled sadly. Then the trained pulled away from the platform with a whisper.

I stood alone on the platform.

I knew I would have to descend the stairwell, re-enter the concourse, and go back to the booth to get another token. It seemed simple enough. I could return, wait for the next train. But the nagging inside me turned into a dread that this had been the last train. As if to emphasize the feeling, a cold, stark wind blew swiftly over the platform, shuffling around scraps of paper and leaves. The stars blinked out one by one leaving the sky black and hollow.

Shuddering, I went to the stairs and proceeded back down into the caverns. The heat rushed up to welcome me. Sweat was soon rolling down my face again. The harsh sounds of grating metal from the lower station were still echoing throughout the concourse. With deep reluctance and growing fear, I continued down the stairs.

My legs felt woodenly unresponsive. The steps, which had been flat and solid, now swayed slightly. They seemed to be spongy. I grasped the railing tightly with both hands to keep from being plummeted to the dark concrete floor below. As I neared the bottom, the metallic shrieks from the lower level grew louder and louder. Above the din I heard strange discordant music.

My heart was beating almost audibly; a large lump started to swell in my throat. The last step tilted to a 45-degree angle causing me to stumble out into the concourse.

The station was empty except for a couple ghostly wanderers drifting about. The singer was still in his spot. He mercilessly struck the guitar strings until they buzzed with bitter noise. I looked at him. He grinned toothily back at me. His eyes were red coals burning brightly in their deep black sockets. Then I realized what song he was singing.

It was AC/DC's "Highway to Hell."

I looked back up the concourse. For some strange reason, I knew it would be useless to try to exit the station the way I had come in. The turnstiles, silent guardians of the station, would block my exit with their unyielding arms. And the blank faced automaton in the booth would merely stare at me.

I looked back at the singer. Without missing a note, he jerked his head in the direction of the lower level. My heart sank, my hands shook. Summoning up my last bit of will, I walked over to the stairwell leading down. The scorching heat was blasting out of the opening with great force. It made me stagger back a step, but I regained my balance. The shrieks and wails from the lower level were rising above tolerable limits causing sharp pains to tear through my ears. I grasped the railing to steady myself. Blisters rose on my hand.

Suddenly, I jumped with a start and whirled to look at a presence that appeared beside me. It was the apparition that had been flickering about he edges of my consciousness all along. She was Destiny, and she was dark. She held out her formless hand. I grasped it. Sadness with a vague sense of relief washed over me as we started down the steps

THE TRAIN
(2007)

Jason stood on the train platform in the lazy light of early evening. Here in the suburbs, the train was above ground, four stretched silverish boxes playing follow the leader for all to see and hear. When it approached the city, it would plunge underground to race through tubes of tile and concrete rumbling the sidewalks above.

The platform was darkened from the footsteps of thousands of commuters passing through this station daily. Dingy white concrete pillars which supported the rigid overhead cover were chipped and marked with names and odd symbols in dark brown spray paint.

The Green Hill Station was deserted except for Jason. The evening was windy warm, pleasant, wafting an odd mix of luscious scents from a nearby restaurant and the familiar subway sourness. He stood at the edge of the platform, for he heard the ringing of the tracks below indicating an approaching train. It was a metallic shearing sound that happened well before the train actually pulled into station.

This was Jason's last trip on the subway. He would be moving away in two days, leaving the city for the wider, open vistas of the arid southwest. He was trading in his straight, perfect canyons of glass, concrete and steel for those of sandstone, rivercut and windblown into dreamish shapes. He wanted to see the city again, to walk the streets again amid the honks and toots of traffic winding its way between silent towers whose inner lights create a Mondrianesque pattern against dark skies.

The rails were loudly ringing now. Jason could look up the track, see the headlights of a rolling behemoth cresting a small hill on its approach to the station. Trains fascinated Jason. Powerful and dense, mighty and fast, they were slow to start, and even slower to stop. They made a lot of noise, even these electrically-powered trains of civilization. They exuded an impressive amount of noise, for it is impossible to move this much mass silently. For all their bluster and bravado, however, trains are limited to a narrow corridor of influence. They must obey their equidistant boundaries. If they don't, they die, usually with spectacular and wrenching results.

The train rolled into the station with a squealish bumble. It stopped beside the platform, heaved a loud sigh and opened its doors. Jason walked onto the vibrating floor inside the train and found a seat near the back end of the car. Air was blowing from the vents that was noncommittal - neither warm nor cold. Its freshness was dubious as well.

There were a few other people in the car. They were scattered among the seats individually. There were no couples or groups, just one here, one there, another over yonder. No one spoke to anyone else, and, as far as Jason could tell, no one even looked at anyone else. Trains or buses can be very much like elevators. Elbows and hips may bump, bodies may inadvertently touch, but minds refuse to connect.

There was another loud sigh. The train made noises as if it grew impatient with waiting. Jason felt a familiar, subtle change in the ubiquitous vibration indicating that preparations were being made to leave this station for the next. The doors began sliding shut when there rose a cacophony of shouts from outside. Jason looked toward the door. A hand appeared in the narrow opening that remained between the closing doors.

The doors sprang open. In leaped an elderly gentleman who looked like he was jumping over a gaping ravine. His hair was mostly white, cropped closely to his head. He sported a large white mustache sprinkled with darker strands giving it a dichromatic appearance. His clothes were worn and faded, but neat. He walked toward the back of the car and sat down in the seat across the aisle from Jason. Jason nodded as the man looked at him while settling in.

The doors closed quickly then, and the train pulled away from the station. It moved sluggishly at first, but soon was rolling on its shiny, smooth tracks at a speed that was both exhilarating and comfortable.

Jason turned to look at the elderly man in the seat next to him. He looked away quickly when he saw the man staring at him. None of the other riders looked his way, so he ignored the man and slumped down into his seat, while leaning against the side of the train.

Jason stared absently out the window, not so much lost in thought as he was mired in momentary observations of the passing landscape. It made him think of hallucinatory experiences with a world rushing by frantically, but one's own sense of captured time standing still inside this pocket of a train car. In the rush, colored lights became drawn out tendrils of neon glow. Buildings next to the track became a blur, yet the rhythmic sway of the train muted any active consideration of such. Jason could feel his desire to think, his will to be soften, melt down into a gelatinous ooze.

Suddenly Jason sat up with a start!

The train was no longer plowing its way through the lazy air of suburbia. It had entered a tunnel. All the sounds of the train were compacted into the relatively small space of the tunnel and hammered at Jason's eardrums.

The train was descending - going downhill at a rapid rate that increased with every minute. He couldn't see ahead, but he knew the feeling. It was like the beginning of the descent down the large first drop of a tall roller coaster.

Jason had ridden this train for years, and he couldn't remember any place in the system where there was a long downward slope.

Maybe the transportation authority was working on the regular tunnels?

Maybe this train had been diverted to a different track due to some incident?

Whatever the reason, the train was rocking wildly back and forth now and going faster faster faster. Jason held on to the seat in front of him to keep from getting thrown onto the floor. Another lurch and Jason felt his stomach rise up into his throat.

The train was no longer on the tracks.

It was free flying through the dark vapors of this subterranean chasm, turning and tumbling about. Jason could sense bottom coming closer, closer, reaching up through the void to grab the train. To smash it against itself. The air was growing warmer, stuffier. Jason wanted to get out of the train car desperately, but the bottom was out there, somewhere, chuckling mercilessly until....

"You don't support the war, do you?"

Suddenly Jason sat up with a start! He opened his eyes, blinked them several times.

"You don't support the war, do you?"

"Huh?" he replied, groggy from dozing.

The elderly man still stared at him. Or maybe he was staring again. He said nothing. Jason felt dislocated, out of phase.

"Support the war?" Jason mumbled a bit irritably. "What are you saying? Why are you asking me this?"

The elderly man sat back in his seat and gazed forward, finally breaking connection.

"You are young. You have not yet seen the likes of what I know." He turned back to Jason. "There are many things in this world that are questionable, but we can't think of the right questions. There are few things that are answerable, but everyone thinks they already knows all the answers."

"So, what of it mister?" Jason continued to grump.

"Do you know that if you take an action, you will never know the results of not taking that action?" the elderly man smiled. "Your actions put into motion things that may or may not have been better left still. Be careful, young man where you place your foot as you take your next step. Ahhh, looks like my station is upon us."

"Have a good rest of your trip," he said, standing as the train approached the Falls Crossing Station. "And make sure you keep your eyes open."

The train slowed and sidled up to the platform, which looked much like the station from which they had left. It came to a stop with a jerk. The elderly man nearly fell over, but his gnarled hands gripped the overhead rail as he shuffled to the door. It opened with a sound of exasperation, and the elderly man disappeared into the evening. Jason watched him disembark with puzzlement. It was an odd way to start a conversation.

Support the war. Support the troops. Jason shook his head. He didn't even know what those statements meant. He could just as easily say that he supported the Rocky Mountains. It would have had as much meaning. War seemed like an inexorable thing to Jason. It was something that would be studied by college history classes a long time in the future. They would be able to look back and determine if it was a good thing or bad. But for now, there were two sides to it, and each side seemed intent on stirring up as much opposition to the other side as possible. Right, wrong, left, right, liberal, conservative.

Jason had a hard time understanding what politics had to do with it all. You either had to send your Army against another army or you didn't. It should be as simple as that. Shouldn't it? He suspected that if the politicians were all put on the front lines with a rifle, most of them would turn tail and run away. They talk big in front of TV cameras and at cocktail parties, no doubt. They wouldn't make good foxhole mates though, and that says something profound.

Yet, the ongoing mantra, support for the war, support the troops. And there were those who said, rather goofily, Jason thought, that they supported the troops, but not the war. It was like saying you support Major League Baseball, but they better not schedule any games. Let's just watch them working out in their uniforms during Spring Training while we drink beer and dream of summer.

His question to them, if he ever met 'them', would be "what do you do to support the troops?" After all, support is a verb. It implies action. Do these people send care packages to the soldiers? Offer financial or emotional support to the families of the deployed. Jason suspected the answer would be "no" to both questions. Most people just talked a lot these days. They didn't really walk.

Jason sighed. The doors closed, and the train pulled away from the station.

"HI!"

Jason was startled by the young, blond head that popped over the seat back in front of him. But he smiled and replied, "Hi, yourself!"

"I'm Andrew! What's your name?"

"Hi Andrew, I'm Jason. Did you get on at the last station?"

"My Daddy's a Army man!" Andrew announced. His eyes sparkled.

"That's great Andrew," Jason replied peering around, a frown forming on his face. "Are you on the train by yourself?"

"You look like a bad man. Why is your face mad?" Andrew asked, his eyes wide.

"Andrew, where is your mommy?" Jason asked a little harshly.

Andrew looked down at the floor. He mumbled, "Mommy's at the next station."

Jason softened his voice. "Hey, that's not far. Why don't you just stay in your seat, or you can sit next to me. That way we'll be sure you get off the train where you should. OK?" He made himself smile the biggest smile he could.

Andrew looked up at Jason and returned the smile. "OK mister Jasey!"

"That's Jason, Andrew, not Jasey."

With an impish look Andrew said, "OK mister Jasey!" With that he turned around and sat in his seat.

Jason blew quietly and shook his head. A child on the train by himself. Where had he come from? Jason didn't see Andrew when he got on the train, didn't see Andrew get on the train. All he could conclude was that somehow he missed Andrew, overlooked him. It was entirely possible that he had been sitting at the far end of the car and moved his way down to Jason's end when he was distracted.

That seemed the most likely answer.

But the fact that a young child was riding the train alone was disturbing. Jason had no children. He had never been married, didn't have a girlfriend at the moment. He didn't even know any children personally. Yet, he felt a cloak of protectiveness fall upon him as he watched the small tow head in front of him bobbing up and down to some nameless tune Andrew was singing.

Jason smiled. Andrew's childlike trust of him was both warming and frightening at the same time. It was far too easy to see how predators would use that trust to their advantage. He shivered at the thought and made a surveillance scan around the train car. Except for a few human forms huddled near the front of the car, there was no one else around.

Jason relaxed. He watched the passing landscape as he listened to Andrew's little concert. More and more lights twinkled on as the remaining vestiges of sunlight shriveled into the distant horizon. A line from the Band's song "Twilight" formed in Jason's mind. "Don't leave me alone in the twilight, 'cause twilight is the loneliest time of day." Jason had no idea what the Band meant by that lyric, but he agreed with it wholeheartedly. There's something about that transitional time when the day grudgingly gives up its light.

It's a bittersweet time that hints at omens and whispers of portents. It's alive with a spirit of urgency for all things temporal; a longing for just a little more day to accomplish, to finish before the big finish. It's a primal feeling. Jason wondered if prehistoric man viewed twilight the same way - as the time to pull all activity back into the cave before the nocturnal predators began slinking about.

Jason's musings of twilight were cut short as the train plunged into the tunnel that began its underground journey below the city. The heart of the city was about 4-6 stops down the line; any stations before then were for the more dense but still residential or industrial areas that fringed the city. They were only seconds now from the Winter Street Station, which is where Andrew said his mother would be waiting. Jason had never disembarked at this station, so he didn't know where to look for the woman. He hoped that Andrew was right and would be able to beeline it to his mother. Then Jason could hop back on the train and head off to his destination.

The train sailed into the station, groaned to a stop, its long aluminum torso lined up neatly with the platform. Jason peered through the windows into the brightly lit, tiled cavern, but he couldn't see anyone waiting on the concrete. With its characteristic sigh, the doors opened to allow passengers to spill out.

Jason stood and tousled Andrew's hair. "Come on mate, we've a mother to find."

Andrew climbed out of his seat and took Jason's offered hand. He seemed quite small to Jason who estimated him to be about 5 years old. Jason shook his head again. They walked out of the train onto the platform.

There was no one waiting anywhere on the platform. In fact, the entire station seemed empty. Jason and Andrew had only walked about 10 feet, when the train heaved a loud breath and the doors closed. Jason spun around only to see it pull away from the platform.

"Hey! Wait!" he yelled, waving his left hand. He stepped toward the train, but it was starting to pick up speed as it dove into the tunnel leading away from the station.

"S'matter mister Jasey?" Andrew asked.

"Oh, nothing," said Jason glumly. "I was going to hand you over to your mother and get back on the train. Now I'll have to wait for the next one to come through."

"Hey! Hey!" A woman's voice echoed through the station.

Jason turned to look where the voice was coming from. On the platform along the eastbound train tracks stood a woman who appeared to be about Jason's age. She was wearing patched jeans and a loose fitting blue t-shirt. Her blond hair was cut short. She looked vaguely familiar to Jason; he didn't know why. He was sure he'd never seen her before, but a feeling of disquiet came over him. Maybe it was simply impatience. Maybe....

"Hi there!" Jason yelled back. "Is this guy yours?" He held Andrew up. Andrew squirmed and giggled while he waved.

"Yes, he's mine! Andrew, where have you been?" Her voice sounded piqued.

"Mommy, mommy! Mister Jasey brought me home," squealed Andrew.

"Look, ma'am. I can't get over there from here. I'll bring Andrew upstairs. We'll meet you there," said Jason.

"OK," she said. Then she disappeared down a corridor that led to the stairs on her side of the station.

Jason lowered Andrew, took his hand, "C'mon kid. You got a date with your mom." He walked swiftly toward the stairs that led up to the world, up to fresh air. Andrew ran alongside him whimpering. Jason ignored him and kept walking.

Andrew tripped and fell, forcing Jason to let go of his hand. He started crying. Jason knelt down beside him.

"I'm sorry little dude. I was in a hurry. Here, do you want me to carry you?" He held out his arms.

Andrew just nodded. He leaned between Jason's arms. Jason picked him up, then climbed the stairs to ground level. There, still holding Andrew, he ripped through the turnstile. He found himself outside the station standing on the sidewalk.

Jason had never been to this part of the city before, so he didn't know what to expect when he came up from below. He lowered Andrew and looked around. It was mostly dark now. The sky must have been overcast, for he could see no stars, just a lamp black void. There were a few streetlights on the street, but their glow seemed ineffectual, merely pooling in small spots on the sidewalk beneath the lights.

The buildings surrounding the subway entrance didn't look like apartment buildings or even business type buildings. They all looked more like warehouses, dark and solemn. There were no cars parked along the side of the street. Jason couldn't see any parking meters either. He turned around and around, but all he saw were the warehouses. They looked like they went on for blocks.

Still looking around, Jason absently said, "Where's your mother, Andrew?" There was no answer.

Jason looked down. Andrew was not where he had set him. Jason spun around; saw no sign of Andrew anywhere.

He ran back into the subway entrance.

"Andrew!" he called down the stairs. There was no sound but the echo of his voice. He glanced back out at the sidewalk and then fumbled in his pocket for a subway token. Thrusting it into the turnstile, he pushed through the triple-armed monopod. It ratcheted slowly at first, then threw him out on the other side. Jason dashed down the stairs to the platform below.

On the platform, Jason slowed up. "Andrew!" he yelled again. The word bounced around the tiled walls and dissipated down the tunnels. Jason, heart racing with worry, contemplated the empty station. He heard the familiar sound of the tracks ringing ahead of an approaching train.

He walked to the edge of the platform, peered down the tunnel. There was a long straight section, and Jason could see the headlight of the train about a half mile away. It was an inbound train, going west to the city.

Jason was tempted to forget about Andrew and just get on the train. He could ride it to the Park Station go into the city hit his favorite pizzeria take a walk through the park maybe go into some stores and reminisce about the years he lived here in this culture of urbanity and theaters and good restaurants and colleges with all the co-ed women he met and....

NO!

But you know how parents are these days, very lax and liberal in their child management, leaving them behind in day care all day while they power-brokered their lives squeezed behind the steering wheels of their BMWs, talking into their hands-free phones as they sip Starbucks and fast forward Sheryl Crow... Andrew probably knew his way home from this station...

NO!

All talk, no walk. Jason looked at his feet. He looked at the train now pulling into the station. Somewhere, there was a 5 year old boy wandering by himself... he should be with his mom or dad. His dad - what did he say about his dad? Something about the Army. The war? Did Andrew say something about that? No, that was the elderly fellow. Andrew shouldn't be alone; his mother was...

OVER THERE! WHAT HAPPENED TO HIS MOTHER??

The train was resting at the platform now, its doors open wide. Jason could see inside. It looked full of people - so strange that the other train had been mostly empty. Jason started pacing back and forth beside the open doors. What were they waiting for? No one was getting on or off.

Then Jason noticed that the commuters were all dressed in some kind of uniform. It looked so very familiar, like those guys who were in the parade riding in their big desert sand-colored vehicles wide and rugged and loaded with danger. As he then remembered looking down on the children by the road waving, running for the tiny pieces of candy he threw, there was light, sound, an earthquake and numbness...

Children.

Andrew!

Jason ran back up the stairs. His heart felt like it would burst out of his chest. He was panting to the point of hyperventilation.

"Andrew!!" He leaped over the turnstile this time, not even bothering to push through it.

Jason skidded onto the sidewalk. It was as deep a night as he had ever seen. The hulking dark warehouses seemed even more ominous than before. They had crept a bit closer to the subway entrance, towered menacingly. Their dull windows revealed a vacancy behind their facade that raised the hair on Jason's neck.

"Andrew!!"

Jason breathed deeply trying to calm his racing heart. He forced himself to become quiet and listen. Nothing. Cupping his hands around his mouth he yelled louder.

"Annnndreeewwwww!!"

Where the subway station echoed, his voice seemed to fall flat among the warehouses.

Then he heard it. Very faint, off to the left somewhere. A small giggle or squeal, he wasn't sure. It was at the edge of his hearing range, almost more imagined than real. But Jason jumped in that direction. He ran for three blocks in a heated craze, coming to a breathless stop when he realized that he had no idea which way to go. He called for Andrew again.

"Mister Jasey, help!" The voice rang out, startlingly clear behind Jason.

He whirled around. There was no one behind him.

"Andrew! Where are you?" he called.

Jason waited. And waited. No response.

He walked back to the last intersection and looked to the left and right. All he could see were more rows of warehouses in either direction, their ill-defined shapes backlit only by a very slightly lighter sky. The streetlights at each corner of the

28

intersection didn't provide much light. Instead, they made him feel exposed more than anything else, so he stood in the shadows away from their meager influence.

Suddenly, Jason saw a movement with his peripheral vision. It was off to the right, there by that car parked at the side of the street. He immediately, instinctively moved around the lamp post to the middle of the intersection and began walking softy in the direction of the movement.

He was troubled by the car parked halfway down the block. In an area of the city where he hadn't yet seen any cars, either driving by or parked, he was suspicious. It was a strange feeling, he knew. Cars are as much a part of the city landscape as pigeons are, but he couldn't ignore a blossoming sense of unease about it.

"Mister Jasey, help me!" The voice leaped out of the darkness ahead of him this time. Beyond the car, the next block down. Jason stiffened.

A high, child-like blood-curdling scream followed the plea for help. The warehouse silhouettes crowded closer to the streets. Jason stared at the car, paralyzed with fear. He had to go to Andrew, but there was something not right about that car. The night turned gooey and liquid. The air and the buildings seemed to warp, to stretch around Jason's concrete legs.

Another scream.

Jason felt a white hot anger rise within him. It exploded his paralysis with molten energy flowing through his muscles.

"Stop it you bastards! He's just a kid!" Jason screeched at the top of his lungs. His legs drove into the asphalt like pneumatic hammers as he sprung ahead with the force of vengeance. Within seconds he was parallel to the car. His arm went up reflexively to the side of his head as if to shield it.

At the same time, the car exploded, lighting up the night and throwing the warehouses into a brief stark relief that revealed them as merely buildings of brick and wood. Empty, perhaps, but nothing more.

Jason was blown off his feet. He landed on his left shoulder and tumbled to the other side of the street. He expected to hear bones snap, or to feel ragged shreds of metal rip into his body, but none of these happened. He lay in the gutter taking inventory of his physical condition.

Across the street, the car burned. Jason raised his head to look.

Standing in the aura of light from the flames was Andrew. He had a big grin on his face as he waved energetically at Jason.

"Andrew?" Jason whispered. He sat up, leaning on one arm.

Andrew skipped over to Jason and flung his arms around Jason's neck. His grip was tight, almost a stranglehold. Jason put his arms around Andrew, sniffed his little boy hair. He held Andrew for years it seemed, reluctant to let go.

"I love you, Andrew." Jason stunned, didn't know why he said that, it just seemed appropriate.

Necessary.

"Love you too, Mister Jasey," said Andrew, letting go and stepping back. He smiled, gave a little wave and said, "Goodbye." Then he started skipping down the street, singing a nameless tune. Andrew disappeared into the darkness, his singing still reaching Jason's ears for a while after. Then there was nothing.

"Goodbye, Andrew," said Jason. He felt strangely peaceful.

He felt as if he had satisfied a spirit of urgency to finish something before the big finish.

Jason stood up, brushed some dirt of his pants and walked back to the intersection. He could see a figure standing under the closest streetlight on the right. The figure seemed to be waiting for him. As Jason drew closer, he could see the elderly man that had spoken with him on the train earlier.

Jason was first to speak. "Sir, how are you? What are you doing here?"

The elderly man chuckled. "You weren't supposed to get off that train."

Jason shook his head. "Huh?"

"You weren't supposed to get off that train."

"I was looking for a lost little kid. I needed to find him, to protect him," he said with an edge to his voice. "His mother was missing; I didn't know where his father was."

"I know," said the elderly man sympathetically. "It's time for you to go back."

Jason didn't move. He stood still thinking about Andrew; wondering why he didn't scoop him up and try to find his mother.

The elderly man was silent for a moment as he looked at Jason, then softly he said, "I will tell you this. Andrew is doing just fine. He is happy and playing and growing. He is a good, young man, free to choose his life's path. His memories will not make him bitter. His mother is also doing well now. She has moved on, but she won't ever forget you."

"Forget me? Why would she even remember me in the first place?" Jason asked. An uncomfortable feeling began forming in his stomach. He seemed on the verge of a realization that threatened to shatter his reality, to make the trip unbearable, if not impossible.

Jason thrust down the feeling vehemently. He swallowed, then said, "Maybe I'd better go back to the train."

The elderly man smiled and nodded.

Jason turned from him and walked back to the station. He arrived at the entrance and took one last look before descending the stairs. The dark warehouses no longer loomed ominous. They were just barren shells in orderly rows, sad and somehow natural, inevitable.

The sky was still starless. There was no moon to brighten up this silent area. Jason walked into the subway entrance, through the turnstile and down the stairs.

The train had not moved from the platform. It sat in the same spot humming not quietly, but not loudly either. The doors were still wide open, just as they were when it first pulled into the station. Jason approached the train. A man in uniform stepped out onto the platform and stood in front of Jason.

"Sergeant Christianson," he stated formally. Then, with a wink, he said, "J.C."

Jason recognized the man as a comrade. As a walker who did very little talking.

"Yes Captain." Jason saluted.

"Come back aboard, J.C. We still have a trip to make," he said returning the salute. "And, by the way, you don't have to salute anymore. We're all equals now, just like we always were." He held out his hand.

Jason smiled, took the Captain's hand, and gave it a firm shake. Then they boarded the train. The doors closed with a sigh.

The train slowly pulled away from the station and disappeared into the tunnel.

THE TRACKS
(2007)

Spring is a woman, Lee thought as he strolled across campus in the early part of evening. Spring is a woman, not because of corny metaphors of new life, rebirth or flowers blooming.

No.

Spring is volatile, full of dreamy warmth one day and cold, violent the next. She sighs, gives you pause for anticipation and makes you think that the wrongness of winter has finally been corrected. Spring soothes sinuses, long since shriveled from dry winter wind, with her amazing array of moist, aromatic breaths. She exudes the earthy fragrances of lilac, fresh soil and pine released from the icy strongbox of February into March. She caresses your face with her taunting, liquid heat. She lulls you into serenity.

Then Spring shrieks madness into your ear as she turns a cold back to you. Her brow darkens. Her chill is a palpable, living thing. Sometimes there's snow, and it drags you back to the cellar from which you just broke free. Waiting, waiting. Or she grabs your hat and throws it across the lawn as she spits at you, threatening to come undone. Her misery becomes yours as you peer through the window watching her sob for days in misty doom.

Eventually, though, Spring returns to good nature. She flirts with you, beckons you to come to her.

And you always eagerly go.

Spring is a woman, thought Lee.

"Her name is April," he said aloud.

"So, have you asked her out?" a voice beside him asked.

Lee snorted, "Yeah. She said she just wanted to be friends. You'd think I asked her to marry me, for crying out loud. It was really weird; she looked real surprised and kind of backed away from me. Listen Geoff; don't tell anyone this, OK?" Lee turned to look at his friend walking beside him.

Geoff shook his head and grinned. "No, I won't tell anyone. But man, she's been staring at you in the library. What's up with that?"

Lee shrugged. "Is she? Was she? I can't tell. Every time I looked at her she was reading or taking notes or something."

Geoff thought about that a minute. "She's pretty crafty, I guess. I've seen her watching. Anyway, what are you doing now? You going to the game tonight?"

Lee frowned. "No, I can't go to the game. I've got two papers due by next Tuesday, and I haven't even started them yet. I'll either be in my apartment or at the library all weekend."

"All right, bro. Too bad, it's gonna be a good one. You sure?"

"Yuh!" Lee said sardonically..

"Hey, no need for terse, man. I'm just looking out for your relaxation welfare," Geoff said with a snicker.

They were stopped at the wide campus gate now, talking under a pale, dull streetlight that had just sputtered on. Lee was tempted to go to the game. He loved watching basketball, and April was a cheerleader for the school team. But her odd rejection of him earlier in the week caused him a little discomfort at the thought of seeing her again so soon.

"Well, if they win tonight, they'll go to the tournament next week. I'll make sure I'm free then. How about we hit the Coffee Mug tomorrow night?"

Geoff gave a sideways glance at Lee. "Suuurre, if you don't have a date with April, that is." He ducked as Lee gave a lazy swing at his head.

"Twit!" Lee said.

"Jerk!" Geoff responded.

"Idiot!" Lee said with a barking laugh that snarled a bit.

"C'mon man, peace!" Geoff held up his right hand.

"Peace, okay. Tomorrow night, then." Lee reached to high-five Geoff's hand. Then he walked off campus into what he jokingly called the real world. He had to walk five blocks to the end of Elm Avenue, cross its intersection with Hancock Street and cut through the parking lot of Kentucky Fried Chicken. This brought him to the parking lot behind an elderly high-rise on Clay Street. Crossing Clay Street, there was yet another parking lot that was shared by Heartland Drug Store and South Shore Liquors. Then onto Olde Colony Avenue where his apartment was located on the second floor of an early twentieth century, 16-unit brick building.

Lee liked this apartment building. This was his first year living off campus. It gave him a sense of independence. The building was located near train tracks which led into the city many miles away. Lee's apartment faced the tracks, so he was able to see trains going back and forth during the day.

The sound of the trains didn't bother him - they weren't all that loud anyway as they were driven by electric motors. But the rhythmic, metallic sound of the great behemoth passing, especially at night, lit up Lee's imagination. He felt like he was living on the threshold of discovery of new and exciting places. He felt like he could step through his door and be whisked away to worlds where he could start anew if he so desired. It appealed to his sense of escape.

It wasn't that he disliked college, or the friends he had there. But lately he was getting a sense of desire to move on in life, to leave the old behind. He was a senior in his last few months of school. After almost four years, Lee had seen everything college life had to offer, and it had grown somewhat stale. He had a subtle sense of wanderlust budding in his soul. That sense echoed most strongly on warm, Spring nights when he could hear the distant hornblow of a train through an open window.

Lee opened the window next to his ratty easy chair and sat down. He felt a balmy breeze breathe its way into his apartment. It was sweet with Spring promises. A little earlier this year than normal; some called it Strawberry Spring. He had no idea where that term originated, but it had been likened to Indian Summer. There were those who predicted more Winter on the way to interrupt the giddy reveries of the fresh season. However, Lee felt deep in his bones that this was the real thing - Spring was actually here. And he was going to enjoy every minute of sensation that it brought. He closed his eyes and breathed deeply, taking in every little nuance of Spring fragrance...

"Lee."

Lee opened his eyes. He thought he heard someone call his name. Perhaps he imagined it. There was no one else in the apartment; he was alone.

"Lee." It was a little louder this time.

Lee jumped out of his chair and looked out the window. His heart shifted into high gear at what he saw.

Standing below his window was April. She was in the weedy area between the apartment building and the fence running along the train tracks. She was looking up toward him with an impish smile on her face.

36

"Ah-ah-ah April?" Lee stuttered. He felt his face flush. "What are you doing here?"

"I wasn't nice to you earlier this week," she began. "I'd like to talk for a while."

Lee felt lightheaded, almost as if he were drunk.

"Sure. Come right up."

"No, not now. Tomorrow night, at the Coffee Mug," she replied. "I'll meet you there at 8:00."

"OK! Wait! I'll be right down," shouted Lee. He raced out of his apartment, down the hall to the stairwell. Leaping down two and three steps at a time, he nearly stumbled but caught himself in time to burst through the front door onto the sidewalk. Then he charged around the apartment building and pulled up to the spot where April stood.

She wasn't there.

Breathing hard both from excitement and the run, Lee whirled around to see if he could spot her walking away. In the gathering twilight, it was difficult to see far. He sprinted to the front of the apartment building. He saw no one walking down the sidewalk or across the nearby parking lot.

"Well, I'll be snookered," Lee said to himself. "How did she get away so quick?"

It didn't seem to matter. He was going to see her tomorrow night. It was a date with April! Lee had been attracted to her since his junior year. Unfortunately, she was dating someone else steadily that year and into this year. But when Lee saw her boyfriend at the Coffee Mug one night with someone who wasn't her, he started asking around. It was Geoff who finally gave him the news he had wanted to hear - April and her boyfriend had indeed broken up for good.

Lee was thrilled. He felt like this was a brand new nickel opportunity, all shiny and pretty. He would finally fulfill his destiny to be with her, to experience her, to take in all her charms as he released his own. He spent most of the school year talking with her when he could – mostly little chitchat. He didn't want to come on too strong, especially since she had just ended a relationship.

April seemed generally friendly, and Lee could see building interest in her eyes. But he played it cool; always open to her when she needed friendship. Always accepting, he listened as she talked about her dating woes, even if it felt like a hot poker piercing his chest when she mentioned other guys. Yes, he was cool because he believed in timing this right, looking for the proper opening that would magically merge the two of them into one entity.

Now, in March, it appeared as if Lee's timing had been pretty good. The rejection when he asked her out came as a shock to him. He thought she was ready. Apparently, though, he had caught her off guard. However, she seemed to be coming around to him a week later. Yeah, he thought, this is the paydirt, the mother lode. This is the it zone, the crunch time, the point where all possibilities come together into a unified whole.

Lee looked at his watch. 7:25 PM. Friday night. The basketball game was going to start soon. Though he hadn't planned on going, Lee reconsidered. It would be nice to watch April bouncing all over the gym floor in her cheerleader mini-skirt, to give her a smile if she happened to glance up at him, make eye contact that fairly crackled with power.

Lee sighed and shook his head. There was too much work to do. Putting off seeing April until tomorrow night would just make their date so much more delicious. He grabbed a book, some note paper and turned on the television for background sound.

Two hours later, Lee set his pen down and leaned back in the chair stretching. He yawned deep enough to make his eyes water. The research for this report was almost complete. He had just one more book to skim through to see if it had any additional information he'd want to include. Grabbing the book from the table, Lee settled back into his chair. He stared out the window into the darkness for a while.

A train rumbled by. Electrical sparks from the third rail punctuated its passage through the darkness. It was northbound – heading toward the city. Lee felt the apartment building shake from the train. It reminded him somewhat of the earthquakes he lived through growing up in California.

Kicking his feet up on the table, Lee started reading the book. But the words blurred into meaningless symbols, and he found his mind drifting to his days in California. It was a carefree time, or so he remembered it as such. Adolescence found its freedom along the railroad tracks in Barstow where he and Janny spent so much time looking for agates and chalcedony as they watched the trains pull away from this hot, desert town bound for who knows where and Janny easily obsessed over things like pretty rocks and tracks that led somewhere else. To someone else? (Janny really shouldn't have let Lee see her talking with Craig earlier that day.) All the while Lee kept his eye on the large dark cloud on the horizon for he'd seen its likes before in the angry flash floods of a few years back, ominous it seemed, almost mushroom-shaped but that's really subatomic particles of quantum field theory reports have to be done by Tuesday after a basketball game and Janny is wearing her cute little cheerleader, doesn't she look like April?

BA-BA-BA BOOM!

Lee's eyes sprang open with a start. Another train was rumbling by his apartment. Lee rubbed his eyes. He peered blearily out the window. What he took for thunder in his dozing must have been the train.

He looked at the train, stiffened, glanced around his apartment and looked again. This train seemed as if it was going backward. It had a blue aura about it that made Lee's mouth open in disbelief. He rose up from his chair, walked over to the window and leaned out.

The train wasn't going backward; it was on the other track heading south. Whatever optical illusion that caused it to look that way must have also caused the blue aura, because it appeared normal now. Lee stepped back from the window and closed it.

He shook his head. He must have still been in a bit of a dream state when the train passed; that was the only explanation that seemed plausible. Lee glanced at the clock on the counter. It said 10:24 - time to put the books away, maybe watch some television and go to bed.

That's when he noticed the television was off. That wasn't right. He didn't remember turning it off. When he started reading the book, he thought he recalled a professional basketball game was playing. But he wasn't sure. Lee picked up the remote control and pushed the power button.

The television burst into life.

"This is a StormCenter Weather Alert. A severe winter storm warning has been posted for the greater metro area. The Doppler radar tracking the storm shows high winds and a huge mass of moisture at its center that can dump up to six inches per hour causing possible white out conditions at times. We should start seeing the first flakes about 12 hours from now. If you don't have to go outside for anything, we recommend you don't. We will now go to our meteorological center for more information..."

Lee sighed. He was sure Winter was finished. He pushed the power button to turn the television off.

The television clicked, the screen blinked. There was a low hum. Then a basketball game sprang into life. It was the same game that was on while Lee was reading. He stared at the remote control and clicked the power button several times. The television turned on and off normally.

Then he surfed through the channels. There weren't many; Lee couldn't afford cable. None of the channels he saw were carrying the weather report.

Lee felt an odd tingling go up the back of his neck. He didn't know what to think. It had been a strange evening. The train in blue, the phantom weather report, even April showing up after he had pretty much given up on her. Deciding there were probably logical answers, but having no idea where to find them, Lee went to bed for the rest of the night.

His sleep was filled with vague, unsettling dreams.

The following day, Lee awoke to a dirty gray sky. The air temperature had dropped about twenty-five degrees from the day before. A chilly ominousness had settled over the area as everyone seemed to keep glancing up in waning hope of seeing the sun.

Lee spent the morning in his apartment feeling listless. He was unable to generate a spark of interest in anything beyond his date with April. After lunch, he willed himself to go to the campus library, so he could research for his second paper. The atmosphere had an electric stillness that defied Lee's attempts to categorize it. On one level, it had the natural feel of an impending storm. On a deeper level, it seemed an extension of the events from the night before. It kept Lee on edge as he walked to the library.

The afternoon was dull, but fruitful. Lee managed to collect most of what he needed for his research paper. Initially, he sat near the entrance, so he could watch to see if April came in. He found the constant door opening and closing distracting, however, so he moved to a study carrel on the second level. Around 5:00, he went to the Student Union for a hamburger and French fries. Then he went back to the library to finish up.

As Lee entered the library building, he noticed snow flakes were starting to fall. Here it comes, he thought glumly as he paused to look up at the sky.

"Oh well, it's only two more hours until D-time," he murmured to himself and went inside. Lee found himself unable to get back into studying with any kind of intensity as the time ticked inexorably closer. Anticipation made him antsy. He was a bit jittery as well. What if April....? Hundreds of "what ifs" flashed through Lee's mind – none of them good.

With nervous energy building in him, Lee found he couldn't sit any more. He looked at his watch; it said 6:58. He decided he'd head to the Coffee Mug now, get there a bit early. Perhaps he could settle down while he waited for April to show up. Lee returned the books to their shelves and threw on his jacket.

The Coffee Mug was a small, local restaurant that appealed to the college population mostly because of its low prices. It was about a fifteen minute walk from the school, even closer to Lee's apartment. For $2 you could order a cup of coffee and a muffin, grilled if you like. It was the perfect date spot, warm, cozy and cheap.

Lee strode with a sense of great purpose to the library door and stopped short.

What he saw through the door made him blink hard. It looked as if someone had taken white paint and covered the glass with it. He burst through the door and was immediately blown back by a sharp wind that covered his face almost immediately with a frozen, wet slush.

The storm was here in full force.

Lee stepped back inside the hall. He wiped the snow vigorously from his face and hair. He stared out at it wondering if he should try to make it to the Coffee Mug. It was either that or go back to his apartment. The distance was about the same.

Then he thought of April looking up at him with her impish smile. Something inside him solidified into defiant steel. He plunged back through the door with no concern for snow or wind or cold.

The wind initially stole his breath, so that he started panting as he went down the stairs to the sidewalk. Turning left he passed through the campus gate back into the real world. Lee kept his head, slightly tilted down, hunched into his jacket. This way the wind didn't hit him smack in the face.

Out on Elm Avenue, it was difficult to see much more than ghostly shapes of houses along the street, or cars swishing by. The streetlights bravely beat a golden glow into the otherwise dark snow that blew as a translucent curtain. Lee could feel bits of the cold mess building up on the back of his collar, dripping onto his neck. He fiercely swept his hand across it to wipe the snow away.

The five blocks of Elm Avenue make for a long walk on a nice day. But on a day like this, it seemed endless. There was no seeing much beyond twenty feet ahead. Now and then the maniacal ballet of snowflakes would slow a bit and open the night up with better visibility. Then the wind would howl back down the street and whip the dance back into its frenzy effectively drawing the curtain closed.

It was during a lull that Lee thought he saw someone walking about a block ahead of him, huddled tight against weather. From the way the person walked, and what appeared to be long, brown hair, he determined it was a woman

"Hey, maybe that's April," he said to himself. "Maybe she has the same idea as me." This idea made him grin foolishly. He decided to stay a distance behind her, not let her know he was there.

He would follow her to the Coffee Mug.

Follow her. Just like the other day across campus. Lee saw her leave the Student Union from a library window. He left to follow her at a discreet distance. To see where she was going. That's all. He was curious, wanted to know more about her likes and dislikes, how she spent her time away from class and study. He thought that told more about a person than anything - what they do in their free time.

So he followed her right down past the greenhouse and the Theatre Arts building. There he had to hang back; there was no place he could stay out of sight. She looked as if she was heading across the parking lot to Memorial Hall which is one of two co-ed dorms on campus. It was the dorm where Geoff lived. No meaning in that. About a thousand other people lived there as well.

"Geoff!" Lee exclaimed out loud. His voice was quickly muffled by scorching wind and swirling snow.

Lee was supposed to go to the Coffee Mug with Geoff, and he had forgotten all about it. Maybe Geoff wouldn't bother venturing out in this storm anyway. Lee should have contacted him, but simply forgot.

The storm paused for a few minutes which gave Lee a good chance to see the woman ahead of him. She was passing under a streetlight as she turned the corner onto Kemper Street. That would take her over to Beale Street which is where the Coffee Mug was located in a row of businesses beyond the Hancock Street intersection.

Her profile looked very much like April. Lee's pulse quickened. Then the storm whipped back to its fury, and she reverted to her ghostly image, barely seen through the driving snow.

Lee felt a rising excitement. He was surer than ever now that he was following April. Following her like he did that evening when she and Darrin (who names their son Darrin these days?) went to his dorm room on the first floor of Memorial Hall. There Lee was able to hide in the hedge under the window of Darrin's room and peer inside.

What he witnessed ripped through his soul like searing acid. He was magnetically fascinated and frantically repulsed by what he saw that night. Then Darrin was at the Coffee Mug two nights later with one of the other cheerleaders, and oh, wasn't it unfortunate the accident he had falling off the subway station platform onto the tracks in front of a slowing train. Those platforms can get real crowded at times and people shove to get in the train first. Just one of those things.

Lee barked a short laugh. He squinted, tried to make out April through the snow ahead. He was following her. He'd find out where she was going. That would tell him a lot about her.

It was becoming more and more difficult to walk; the snow was getting so deep. Lee's toes were growing numb; he had worn sneakers that day. He kept trudging along though, hardly noticing his discomfort as he stared intently ahead.

She was now at the intersection of Beale and Hancock. It was a large intersection, usually very busy with traffic. Tonight though, the traffic lights turned green, yellow, red in vain - there was no one to obey them. The darkness of Elm Avenue and Kemper Street with their towering trees was replaced by the mystical aura of streetlights at each corner. Most of the businesses along both streets were closed, but they usually were at this time of day anyway.

Lee watched April cross the intersection. He wondered what she was up to. The Coffee Mug was on the other side of the street. She looked as if she was going to walk past it. Lee decided to try and catch up to her, maybe get some answers.

"Hey! April!" he yelled. It went nowhere, all caught up and muted by the dense snow wall that separated them. He started walking faster, his sneakers kicking up clods of snow. It was ankle deep now on the sidewalk which made movement difficult. But no matter how much harder he walked, he couldn't seem to catch up to her.

She ghosted in and out of sight through the veiling snow. The buildings on either side of the street were mere suggestions of shape. Lee couldn't even see across the street but he knew they had walked past the bank which was across from the Coffee Mug. Yet April had not stopped. Had not entered the destination she had laid out to him the day before.

Lee was starting to grow angry. He was cold, his feet were numb, and he had no idea where April was going. She wouldn't stop to wait for him; she always stayed just within his range of sight.

"She's going to pay for this," he said through chattering teeth. She seemed to be cutting through the Heartland Drug parking lot. It had turned into a vast, empty snowfield by this time, barely lit by ineffective lighting. April was a dark smudge against a slightly lighter night snow backdrop.

Lee stopped. It just occurred to him where they were. It appeared that April was going back to his apartment. So much the better, he thought, shivering as the icy wind blew around his face

"We can have some real fun there, eh?" Lee snorted to himself. Then he noticed that she had stopped as well. He stared hard, shielding his eyes from the snow, and tried to see what she was doing.

He wasn't absolutely positive, but she seemed to be beckoning to him.

Lee grinned, felt the ice chunks that had built up in his mustache. He jumped forward, started running and flailed his arms wildly about as his feet threatened to slide out from underneath. He managed to keep his balance as he jogged along, slipping on random ice patches under the snow.

She, too, continued on, disappeared into the grove of trees that grew along Old Colony Ave. When Lee reached the grove, he looked for her footprints, but it was too dark to see much of anything. Walking carefully with his frozen hands extended ahead of him so as to not run into a tree, he navigated his way through the grove without mishap.

When he came out the woods onto Old Colony Ave, Lee paused to see if he could see April anywhere. But the snow was falling even harder now, if that was possible, and he was unable to see beyond five feet. He spun around, lost in this dim world. He knew his apartment wasn't far, but didn't know which way to go. He was near home, yet he was lost.

"Leeeeee," the wind howled his name.

"Leeeeee!!" it shrieked away to his left.

"Lee," a breath of almost a whisper seemed so close that he jerked his head around.

"April?" he whispered.

"Lee, this way," Lee stumbled on stiffened legs in the direction of the voice. He still held his hands out as if blind.

"Where are you, April?" he shouted.

"This way, Lee. Follow my voice."

Lee plodded through snow that came almost up to his knees. His feet were like blocks of wood; he was sure there would be frostbite to deal with. He struggled up a small rise, then felt the ground drop away beneath him. He almost stumbled, went down with a cry of pain on one knee. Then, just as quickly as the world fell out from below, he was back on level ground.

"April!" he cried out.

"Over here, Lee. Just a little way left to go." Her voice had an odd hollow tone.

Lee stepped forward and immediately found himself face down in deep snow. He had tripped over something hard and unyielding. Muttering, he pushed himself back to standing, took two more steps and tripped again. Before he could get up this time, he sensed someone standing near him. He peered up; the face was shadowed in darkness.

"April? Is that you? What do you think you're doing?" Lee raised himself up and brushed the snow from his clothing.

The figure didn't answer.

"APRIL! WHAT ARE YOU DOING?!" Lee screamed.

The figure stepped closer. Lee could finally make out the face.

The hair on the back of his neck stood straight out. The blood in his veins turned to ice.

"J-J-Janny? J-J-Janny?" It was all he could think to stutter.

A wry smile spread across her face, but her eyes were empty. "Yes, Lee. It's me, Janny! Ta da!" she said in a sing-song way.

A fit of shivering slammed Lee, His eyes bulged out.

"JANNY! IT CAN'T BE YOU! I WATCHED..." he swallowed hard, "I WATCHED...."

"Yes, Lee," Janny said calmly. "You watched me die. You watched me get hit by that train when we went looking for rocks by the tracks..."

"BUT HOW...., WHERE?" Lee's mind was swirling. It had gone blank; he couldn't think of anything to say or ask.

"Oh, right, Lee... you didn't just watch me get hit, did you?" There was an edge to her voice now.

"Uh-uh-uh-uh," he started to cry. Guilt, fear, loneliness, frostbite; Lee was overwhelmed.

Janny continued, "You pushed me in front of that train, Lee. Now I've come to return the favor. You are on these tracks, and you are alone. Look behind you." She peered over his shoulder.

Lee snarled, "NO!!! I'M NOT GOING TO LOOK, JANNY! THERE IS NO TRAIN! THE TRACKS ARE COVERED WITH TOO MU..."

He never finished his sentence. There was a terrible squealing of wheels and a horrific thud. Had he looked, his last sight would have been of a train enveloped in a blue aura.

****

"So, you were supposed to meet Lee here too?" Geoff said with incredulity. April nodded and smiled. Her dimples always drove Geoff crazy.

"Yes, I was going to talk with him... let him know about....
us," she said as she reached her hand across the table to touch
Geoff's hand loosely wrapped around a coffee cup. "I wanted to
be gentle about it. Not let him down hard. Know what I mean?"

Geoff gazed at her face. Her long brown hair billowed
softly down over her shoulders, sweetly framing her face and
accenting her deep brown eyes.

"Yeah, I know what you mean. I don't know what it will do
to our friendship. He really has a thing for you."

April's face grew serious. "He scares me Geoff. He's
always staring at me." Her voice dropped to a whisper.

Geoff looked at his watch. 8:46.

"Well, he's apparently not going to show up. We'll deal
with this later. Let's head back to the school and find a dark,
quiet corner somewhere."

"OK, hon. Sounds like fun," she purred.

They rose and went out the door of the Coffee Mug. It was
a wondrously warm Spring night. Geoff breathed deeply the
sensuous air and sighed with contentment. Strawberry Spring
they had been calling it. He didn't care what name they had for
it – it was going to last forever. He could feel it in his bones.

Geoff put his arm around April, pulled her close. She
snuggled into him as they walked slowly down the brightly lit
sidewalk, talking softly.

Behind them, a train's wheels squealed as it rumbled
through the tunnel under Beale Street, heading for the city.

A BRAVE NEW WORLD
(2008)

"Hi Grandpa!" Billy shrieked with a big grin on his face.

"Hi Billy! How are you doing?" I answered patting the seat beside me. He sat down. I put my arm around him and gave him a big squeeze. At ten years old, he's a bit too big to put on my lap.

I miss those days.

"I'm doing good, Grandpa."

"Great, great Billy. What's the news?"

"Well, I was on YouTube yesterday, and I saw the most awesome video"

"What is YouTube, Billy?"

"It's a place on the internet where you can go watch videos people make, Grandpa."

"Oh, like home movies? Isn't that boring?"

"No Grandpa. It's great! Like yesterday, I watched the best guitar master in the world."

"Oh really? Now you know, I play some guitar, don't you? I wouldn't say I'm a master, but I used to be in a pretty good band when I was younger."

"Grandpa," Billy frowned, spoke in a somewhat scolding voice. "I'm not talking about that. I'm talking about the video game Guitar Master."

"Oh," I replied, properly chastised. "So they made a video game out of playing guitar? How does that work?"

"You take the guitar that comes with the game and you play along with the band in concert. If you do good, they cheer for

51

you and you get points. If you do bad, they boo you and you lose points."

"Heh, sounds like fun. What kind of guitar do they include in the game... acoustic? electric? Fender? Gibson? That must make it an awfully expensive game!"

Billy laughed, "Oh Grandpa, you're so silly."

"Oh? How so?"

"It's not a real guitar. It's a game guitar. You play it by pushing down the buttons the game tells you to push down."

"Buttons? What about strings?"

"There aren't no strings, Grandpa."

"So, let me see if I understand you correctly. There's a game about playing guitar with a band, but you don't have to really know how to play guitar? How many buttons are there....?"

"There's only five buttons."

".... ah, five. And the game tells you which buttons to push? And if you do it right, I suppose that means in a particular sequence, then you get points. And this guy on YouTube.. err, what's his name?"

"Ace Frack, Grandpa."

"OK, this Ace Frack is a guitar master because he pushes buttons the game tells him to push?"

"That's right, Grandpa. Ace has fans all over the world."

I smiled at Billy, "Great, great Billy. You do realize he's not really playing an instrument, right?"

Billy became a bit exasperated again. "Grandpa, he's the guitar master!"

I saw no reason to go further down this road, so I changed the subject.

"What else do you watch on the internet, Billy?"

He thought for a moment. Then his eyes lit up and he said, "Have you ever heard of Dogs of War, Grandpa?"

"Oh yeah Billy.. that was a movie back in the '80s with, ummm, let's see, it was just on the other night on AMC.. wait, Christopher Walken and Tom Berenger. Good movie, that."

"No, no Grandpa. It's a website where you can go fly fighter jets and shoot down other fighter jets."

"Ahh, a flight simulator. They use those to train real pilots, Billy. Did you know that?"

"No Grandpa, that's cool," Billy rushed on. "On Dogs of War there's a video of Zack Barley shooting down his 920th kill. He's a Supreme Ace. He got an International Distinguished Aces Gold Medal for it. He's wicked awesome!"

"Hmmm, 920th, eh? Billy, did you know your great Uncle Warren was a Vietnam War pilot? In fact he was an ace, and he won the Medal of Honor."

This grabbed Billy's attention. "Cool Grandpa. How many planes did he shoot down? 1000?"

I chuckled. "No Billy, he shot down eight."

"Eight, Grandpa?" Billy frowned again. He seemed disappointed.

"Yeah, well you only need to shoot down five to be considered an ace."

"Well Zack shot down 920."

"It's not easy to do in real life, Billy." I gently tried to convince him.

"Zack set a record by shooting down twelve in less a minute."

I didn't quite like the way this was going either, so I moved the subject along.

"That's nice, Billy. Say did you hear about David Ortiz?

He hit two home runs in the game last night against the Yankees."

Billy loved the Red Sox. And David Ortiz was his favorite player. But it didn't seem to excite him. Instead he seemed to be searching for something deep in his brain. Then he smiled.

"Grandpa!"

"Yes, Billy?"

"I was playing MLB 2005 the last week, and I hit five home runs in a game!"

"Is this one of your video games too, Billy?"

"Yeah, Nintendo GameCube. Do you think I could be a major league baseball player some day?"

I just sighed and patted his head. He doesn't even play Little League.

"Maybe some day Billy. Maybe some day."

"Awesome!"

OVERHEARD AT THE GAME
(2007)

He was always there and never at a loss for words.

He sat in the same spot each time, end of the bleachers near the dugout, three rows up. He always wore the same John Deere baseball cap and light green jacket with faded grease stains on the front. He would always give a wink and a smile when I walked over to him.

I never found out his name or who belonged to him. It didn't seem to matter.

One of the common greetings at the beginning of the season was, "Which one is yours?"

Usually, the person who was asked would smile and reply, "Cody"

"Tyler"

"Andrew"

Any name that was popular for the time would fit. If that person was particularly gregarious, he or she might point to third base, right field, pitcher, or wherever their Cody, Tyler or Andrew was playing at the time.

But I never asked him the question, "Which one is yours?" Like I said: it didn't seem to matter. He was a regular. He was into the sport. He knew who all the kids were, and he could talk about every one of them, the position they played, how they were doing with a bat and glove.

"Now watch Isaiah, the pitcher," he said. "He's got a good arm, but he's wild, got no control. Your Kevin should do OK against him if he doesn't get intimidated. He's got patience at

55

the plate, unlike some others who either don't swing at all or swing at everything that's thrown."

I replied, "Kevin's really getting an eye for the pitches. He just needs to swing through better and figure out how to place his shots."

"Oh, ayuh, but that will come with time," a smile and a wink.

I returned the smile, gave a nod and wandered over to the trio of guys standing between the bleachers and dugout. I didn't join them; just stood a couple feet behind and listened.

"Didja hear the Yankees signed Clemens?"

"Oh yeah, saw it on the news this evenin' before comin' over."

"Twenty-eight mill for half a season - ain't that the end all?"

"Well Steinie's gotta do sumthin'. They ain't had consistent pitchin' for years now, least not since 03."

"I don't know they wuz real consistent then."

"Well they did get into the World Series, don't that say something?"

"You think the Sox should be worried?"

"Nah... wait, wait, you see that? The ump called that a strike! It musta hit the dirt three times before it made the plate!"

"Little League umps, man, eh .... "

All the while I could hear the coaches from each side yelling to their respective players...

"Move out deeper, Brandon. Two steps to your left!"

"Just get it over the plate, Isaiah, don't worry about the runners!"

"Don't swing at the high ones, Jacob!"

"Good eye, Jacob!"

"Austin, watch your man on second!"

And so on. It's the same thing every game. A litany of shouted instructions throughout the entire six innings.

Meanwhile, I sauntered behind the bleachers to the far end and stood quietly. A couple of mothers were cloistered there.

"So Frankie has to do his history report AND the science project AND a paper on global warming for English all this week."

"Global warming for English? Shouldn't they be doing that in science?"

"Well they made the English class watch the movie, I can't say why."

"Ryan did his report last week, and he's almost done with the science project. How'd Frankie get behind."

"You didn't know? Chickenpox."

"Oh dear, well it's good he got that out of the way now."

"I s'pose, but the teachers aren't cutting him any slack."

"No, they don't do that these days."

"No, they don't, especially with standards testing coming up."

"Oh, when is that?"

"It's in two weeks."

"I swear, Ryan, never tells me a thing."

"I have to pry it out of Frankie, too, thank God they email announcements out now."

"I didn't know that. How....."

Suddenly a cheer arose from the bleachers of the opposing team. I didn't know what happened, but the teams were switching, which meant it was the bottom of the inning.

And the coaches yelled.

"Hurry, let's get moving!"
"Get out to the field!"
"Here, take these balls!"
"Kevin, move over to shortstop, Jacob, switch with Kevin!"

Standing a bit to the left of the bleacher was a town selectman, whose son played first base, and another parent. I could hear bits of what they were saying.

"C'mon Stevie, why can't I get that variance?"
"Brad, you know it wasn't grandfathered in. You need to go to the Planning Board and get it started."
"Steven, you know they'll turn me down. Hank's always had it in for me since that right of way issue two years ago."
"Well Brad, we have ways of doing things. We can't change that."
"You could if you wanted to."
"What, amend the charter?"
"No, no, not so drastic. Just have a talk with Hank."
"Hmmm, maybe I'll do that."
"Hey Stevie, great, nice work on that green zone thing, by the way."
"Yeah, thanks, that took a lot of effort, I...."

I thought I saw Brad hand Steve something surreptitiously, but I couldn't be certain.

I was standing at the end of the bleachers for the visiting team. The "visiting" team is in the dugout beside the third base line, and the "home" team is on the first base side. Neither team actually goes anywhere; they play in the same field on the same road for every game. The designations "home" and "visiting" just determine who gets to bat first.

The bleachers are small, rough wooden stands beside the dugouts that rise up to eye-level, so when you walk behind them, you can stare at a row of rear ends if you like.

I decided to go to the concession stand located behind the backstop.

On the way, I walked around the back of the bleacher for the visitors. A middle-aged husband was sitting on the top row beside his wife. I heard him say...

"What's up with that over there?"

"S-s-s-s-s-h! Keep your voice down. Over where?"

"There in the lawn chairs."

"Oh, you haven't heard?"

"Heard what?"

"She left her husband for that woman she's sitting beside."

"Nooooo?"

"Yeah, that's what Barbara told me the other day."

"Wow, do you think they'll kiss?"

"Oh stop that! And don't stare!"

"I'm not staring... but I still don't get it."

"Get what?"

"She's a looker, why hook up with another woman?"

"Well, that's what Barbara said. She also said...."

And so it went.

I could hear and smell grilled meat, you know, burgers, hot dogs, sausage. Sonny was doing the grilling today as well as running the concession. As I stepped into line he was saying to a customer in front of me...

"I love doing this. I'm thinking about setting up a stand in town for the summer. Tourists always stop at hot dog stands. Here ya go buddy! That's four dollars for the hot dog and chips. Who's next?"

"Hey Sonny, serve me up a sausage dog, would ya?" I asked moving up.

"Absolutely, want a soda to go with that?" he said.

"Yeah sure," I replied. "Bag of Doritos too, if you don't mind."

"Excellent choice, if you don't mind my saying!" Sonny was a tall, outgoing fellow with a goatee and large stomach. He looked as if he could be a chef on a cable cooking show. He handed me a sausage in a club roll, hot off the grill and garnished with sauteed peppers and onions. The sweet smell of cooked onion brought back memories of county fairs in the fall. They were only about three months away, but now was mid-Little League season – no reason to think about autumn yet.

"And the price comes to $5.50, sir," Sonny said, handing me the chips and a cold can of Coke. I gave him a five and a one, told him to keep the change. Sonny was a disabled veteran. Not many people know that.

"Thank you muchly," he said smiling.

I said nothing in return, just waved. My mouth was already filled with a large bite of the sausage.

Walking behind the backstop, I passed a woman who was complaining to the fellow standing next to her...

"Did you see what the coach just did?"

"Hmm? Ah, what's that?"

"He stopped the game to make the batter tuck in his shirt!"

"Oh? And what's wrong with that?"

"Well why would he do that? What difference does it make if his shirt is tucked in or not?"

"They ARE called uniforms, ya know."

"So? He embarrassed Isaiah in front of everyone."

"Isaiah's a punk anyway, thinks he's God's gift to baseball.... and he ain't."

"That doesn't matter; it's still not right."

"Don't you understand what the coach is doing?"

"No, what is he doing?"

"First, there is a uniform rule in Little League. He is enforcing that. Second, he's trying to get in Isaiah's head."

"What do you mean?"

"He's trying to rattle Isaiah, affect his play. It's a pretty smart move if you ask me."

"Well, it still isn't right, and I'm going to complain."

"Beth, save your lawyerin' for the court, OK?"

"Well, there's no reason for you to say that."

"Beth, it's just a game, and it's played in more ways than one. You should know that. Besides, Isaiah ain't even yours."

"It's just not right to embarrass him....."

On and on it went. I moved out of earshot.

Around the ballfield, you can always pick up snippets of conversation like that....

"My son told the coach he wanted to pitch, but the coach won't let him."

"My son isn't getting enough field time."

"I don't like the way the coach conducts practice. I don't think the kids are learning anything."

"The coach always lets his son bat lead off and no one else."

"They have too many practices. We're busy people."

And so it goes.

I don't agree with most of those discussions. I find the coaches to generally be even-handed and reasonable. Sure, favoritism is played sometime; I guess that's to be expected, and as long as it doesn't become blatant what can you do except force your kid to quit? I used to argue, try logic and reason with these people. However, most of them won't be satisfied no matter what.

I finished the sausage and Doritos behind the home team dugout, threw the trash into a nearby 50-gallon drum refuse can swarming with yellow jackets and flies.

There's nothing like a good sausage or hot dog at the baseball field.

Nothing, unless you count playing baseball on a warm, clear summer evening where fresh breezes keep the skin cool and dry. Or nothing unless you are young and wearing the same uniform for the third year in a row along with most of your teammates who have grown, trained and developed into a competent team.

My son, Kevin, had been on the Smithfield Oil & Gas Tigers for three years now. He and about seventy-five percent of the other kids on the team came up from the minor leagues all at the same time, so the Tigers had been able to build a core of players that not only developed individually, but as a team as well. They were the best team in the league, but it took a couple years of dust, sweat, defeat and tears to hone them.

A cheer erupted from the home team bleachers. I wandered in that direction to see what had happened. As I passed behind the home dugout, I could hear the coach saying, "OK guys, get your rally caps on. We're hitting now. Joey, keep your eye on the ball!"

The bleachers were buzzing with talk...

"Joey wasn't sure if he wanted to play this year or not. It was between this and lacrosse; it's the school's first year for lacrosse..."

"Joey, don't swing at those high ones!"

"Yeah, Mikey's gonna miss two games in June. We will be in Vermont then. It's the only time I could get off this year..."

"I read that chapter, ha, hah, hahahaha, it was funny..."

I walked to the far end of the bleacher. Joey must have struck out, for when I popped around the end, he was no longer batting, nor was he on base. Some kids spend their whole season striking out.

Or walking. They never get a hit.

The batter's box is one of the scariest places to be in Little League. Most pitchers have nominal control over their pitches, and the possibility of getting beaned by a ball traveling 375 miles per hour is quite intimidating.

There were two younger guys, I'd say late twenties, standing about six feet from the end of the bleacher and engaged in a quiet conversation. They both wore sunglasses and had similarly styled hair – the power coif is what I like to call it, wavy and perfect, unable to move in wind. They looked too young to have children old enough to play in this league, so their presence was a mystery to me. I could only hear pieces of what they were saying, and even then, I wasn't sure who said what without actually watching them talk...

"....tossed her out..."
"...found... stash...."
"...snacked(?).. mouth.... quiet...."
".... hi (or high)... work...."
"....scan (scam?).... get myself some..."

I found it vaguely disquieting. I turned to them and said, "Great ballgame, huh?"

They stopped talking, looked at me. One piped up and said, "Yeah, they're doing really well."

Then they sort of shuffled about fifteen feet farther from the bleacher than they had been and resumed their private conversation. I turned back to the game. The bleachers on the visiting side of the field had burst into cheer, and I saw the teams switching places again, which meant a new inning.

I said hello and made small talk with the few parents I knew from the home team. Then I decided to go back to the other side of the field. Navigating the conversational kaleidoscope, I made my way behind the bleachers, dugouts and backstop...

"$150 for a bat? Wow!"

"We aren't going this year..."

"Two hot dogs, chips and a Mountain Dew."

"I told him he needed new shoes, but..."

"Ball three. Three and one."

"Darryl bought me the nicest ring for our anniversary..."

"Do you know how many workshops the teachers had this year?"

"No."

"Yes."

"I don't know."

"Corey, stop digging holes in the field!!"

He was still sitting there in his John Deere baseball cap and light green jacket. He saw me approach, gave me a wink and a smile as I approached the visiting team's bleachers.

He said, "Your Kevin is doing a great job at shortstop."

I smiled. Kevin always does a great job at shortstop.

"Yeah, he loves that position. Mind if I sit with you?"

"Not a problem, come right up," he said sliding over.

I climbed up and sat down beside him. We never introduced ourselves, but it didn't seem to matter. We watched the game and talked about it to the end.

THE SIX O'CLOCK NEWS
(1994)

Doug: "Good evening. I'm the clean cut Doug Whiteteeth and this is the effervescent Paula Goodbody here with the evening report on the Annual Holiday Mall Super Bowl.

Tonight we will be going to our reporters in the field to give us the latest update on the stiff competition growing in the area malls. But first, this special report by Paula."

Paula: "Thank you, Doug. We spoke with store managers this morning during the pre-opening warm-ups. They are optimistic that this season will show a new consumer confidence in spending. While very little hard cash is actually being handed off, sales receipts indicate that the credit card is making a strong rebound. This is not a surprising development since most shoppers' cash is tied up in taxes, and the credit companies have put payments on waivers during the holiday season.

As paychecks and savings accounts fizzle out by halftime, we favor Visa and MasterCard in the second half with an exclusive showing in the final quarter. Back to you, Doug."

Doug: "Thank you, Paula. The Annual Holiday Mall Super Bowl is a festive time for all participants. To capture the spirit we have sent ace reporter, Clyde Misscue, to the Park Avenue Mall to describe the atmosphere. Over to you, Clyde."

Live remote video signal replaces studio newsroom. We see Clyde's snarling face turned to the right, microphone in his left hand. We hear him faintly saying, "Keep your kid away from me lady or he's mincemeat."

Doug: "Clyde, can you tell us what it's like out there? . . . Clyde?"

Clyde turns toward the camera looking somewhat startled. He quickly composes himself with a broad, warm smile.

Clyde: "Hi Doug. We have a capacity crowd here tonight; the biggest I've seen in a long time. You can almost smell the excitement in the air. The managers have been training their sales teams all year for this huge event, and they look like they are ready for the task.

We kicked off the evening with the traditional, sacred holiday anthem - Santa Claus is Coming to Town. From that point on it's been pure pandemonium."

Doug: "Clyde, what do they have for decorations?"

Clyde: "Doug, the entire place is festooned with banners, foil snowflakes and decorated, aluminum fir trees. In the center of the mall there's a twenty-foot Frosty the Snowman, and this year they added a special touch. A tape loop has been placed in Frosty to enable him to say, "Peace on earth" over and over again. It's a real holiday paradise here, Doug. It's very touching."

Doug: "Thank you, Clyde. Happy Holidays to you."

Clyde: "Thank you, Doug. Happy Holidays to you and all our viewers."

Clyde quickly turns and yells, "That's it kid! I'm coming after you!" He throws down his microphone and runs away from the camera, chasing what appears to be a shrieking ten year old boy. A woman, laden with large packages, immediately flashes across the scene and, cursing, frantically takes up pursuit. The scene goes black.

The studio newsroom comes back up.

Doug, chuckling: "Emotions seem to be running high this year. Is it any wonder? The hottest new toy of the season, Macro Universe, Cosmic Defender of the Inter-Galactic Champions of Justice and Master of Voodoo, complete with plastic laser ray water pistol and lifelike rubber chicken, is selling out everywhere you turn. More on this story from correspondent Alicia Babbelon."

Cut to Alicia. She is standing in front of a store that has a large sign over the entrance proclaiming, "You are now entering Wonderland Toys." Two 4-foot teddy bears pirouette on both sides of the sign. There are so many people crowded at the entrance that you cannot see inside the store.

Alicia: "Thank you, Doug. As you can see, the entrance to Wonderland Toys is literally clogged with people as they struggle to buy the last Macro Universe, Cosmic Defender of the Inter-Galactic Champions of Justice and Master of Voodoo, complete with plastic laser ray water pistol and lifelike rubber chicken. The manager of the store has kept the toy in a steel vault behind the counter all day, and he will bring it out in a few minutes. At that point the competition will begin and one lucky person will take that toy home."

Doug: "Alicia, do other stores have any of these toys left?"

Alicia: "Doug, no they don't. At last report, all stores in the state sold out in the first few days. That's why competition is so tough here. There are people who traveled over three hundred miles for this last toy, and they refuse to be denied."

A loud siren suddenly cuts into the report. Alicia starts yelling and jumping up and down. The crowd surges as a tidal wave, and the camera begins jiggling violently. Then the screen goes black.

The studio newsroom comes back up.

Paula: "Please stand by. We are having technical difficulties. Doug, what do you think happened?"

Doug: "Paula, I'm not sure. Once we reestablish our connection, Alicia can fill us in. In the meantime, some news from around the world. Paula."

Paula *(speaking quickly)*: "Thank you, Doug. Major earthquakes hit Mexico, China and Pakistan. The president of South Africa was assassinated. The Nikkei Stock Market crashed. Israel is at war with Saudi Arabia, Jordan, Syria and Iran. And now, back to Alicia."

Alicia is still standing in front of the store. Her hair is mussed up, and she has a black eye. A trickle of blood spills from a cut on her lip. In the background, people are being carried away on ambulance stretchers. The storefront is demolished. One of the pirouetting teddy bears is missing.

Alicia: "Thank you, Paula. As you can see quite a struggle took place here. One customer emerged victorious, however, and he is standing here beside me surrounded by armed security guards."

She turns to the customer. He is cordoned from the rest of the shoppers by six burly men wearing .44 magnum revolvers on their hips.

Alicia: "Could you tell our viewers your name and address?"

Customer: "Um, I don't think that would be a good idea."

Alicia, chuckling: "No, I guess not. Well, tell us about your amazing feat."

Customer: "Well, they're just regular feet, size 10. I got a few corns on 'em."

Alicia: "No, no. I mean tell us about what just happened. You know, how you got the last Macro Universe, Cosmic Defender of the Inter-Galactic Champions of Justice and Master of Voodoo, complete with plastic laser ray water pistol and lifelike rubber chicken."

Customer: "Oh that. I had a good feeling today. I just came back from a long layoff, and I was ready to get back into the game. When the siren went off I saw an opening, and I dove through it. Then I saw daylight, and the toy was right there. So I grabbed it."

Alicia: "That's great. Did you do any special training for this event?"

Customer: "Yeah, I watched the Jane Fonda workout video every day in my living room for a week."

Alicia: "Who is the lucky child that will get that priceless treasure for a Holiday gift?"

Customer: "Oh, I don't have any kids. I'm gonna auction this off on Holiday Eve and make a bundle."

Alicia: "Well that about wraps it up here, Doug. Back to you."

The scene switches to the studio newsroom.

Doug: "Whew. And they say there's no more entrepreneurial spirit in America any more. Ladies and gentlemen, we were just handed a special bulletin. It seems that a dangerous, subversive group of nuts were arrested in the mall just a few minutes ago. It is alleged that they were singing the archaic Christmas carol, Silent Night, and this, of course was disrupting the events. We will have more on that for you as the information comes in."

Paula: "I hope they get the book thrown at them, Doug. Wackos like that can destroy perfectly good family holidays."

Doug: "That's right, Paula. Well, that's it for tonight's evening news. Be sure you tune in at 7:00 tomorrow morning for the retailers' tallies of today's sales. And from our news station family to you, goodnight and Happy Holidays."

UNCLE LEO'S NOSE
(2007)

Uncle Leo had a big nose.

My mom, Leo's sister, preferred to call it aquiline. She'd say it's a strong, aquiline nose that he'd inherited from his Aunt Estelle, and he should be proud of it. I never knew what she meant by that until I looked up the word "aquiline." Then I discovered that it was just a nicer way of saying "a really big nose."

Many people would comment about Uncle Leo's nose, some behind his back, some right to his face. They'd call it a honker, schnozzola or schnoz for short. He'd be called Pinocchio, Cyrano or Jimmy Durante. One person even said that Jimmy Durante would be jealous of Leo's nose.

Uncle Leo took it all in stride, at times even laughing at a rude comment that would hurt someone else's feelings. It never seemed to bother him. When I was 15 years old, I asked him a question.

"Uncle Leo, why don't you get a doctor to trim some of that nose back? They can make it look really good these days."

He just eyed me quizzically and replied, "Jimmy, this nose is a gift. It saved my life."

I was taken aback. "How'd it do that Uncle Leo? "

Leo chuckled and said, "You ain't old enough yet Jimmy. But I'll tell you one day."

Since he wouldn't tell me the story, I figured that he probably sniffed out a fire and got out of the building before it burned down. But when I asked my mom about it, she said she didn't know. I never failed to ask him about it whenever I saw him. He always came back with the same reply.

"You ain't ready Jimmy."

As the years went by, Uncle Leo's nose seemed to grow even larger, if that was possible. Yet it didn't perturb him in the least. If anything, Leo became more serene and accepting of it.

I secretly envied his good cheer. I found it increasingly difficult to be cheerful of anything as I grew older. By the time I was 46, I was in my third marriage, and that was beginning to teeter towards failure. My teenage son and daughter from my first marriage no longer spoke to me. I couldn't blame them. I had left their mother for a younger woman who I'd hired as a claims adjuster for my growing insurance company. I thought I had everything; a thriving business, an exciting, new relationship with a gorgeously sexy woman. It felt like a reprieve from some indeterminable prison sentence I had been serving.

Unfortunately, as it would turn out, the sense of well-being was illusory and short-lived, for my new wife had been dating one of the salesmen in my company when we met. She apparently started doing so again after we married. I immediately fired both of them, and they promptly filed a lawsuit against me for wrongful termination. They ultimately lost their suit, but it cost me a lot of money in attorneys' and court fees.

I was able to get the marriage annulled. Somewhere in the mess of lawsuits, annulment and the general chaos of my life, I started drinking heavily. I'd had a tendency to be a somewhat vigorous social drinker anyway. It never seemed to affect my business decisions; life was pretty good. But when things went bad I sought out alcohol like a hungry man seeks out food. I became withdrawn, sullen. I spent my days at work, if I went in, either drunk or hung over. It all had a detrimental effect on business. I could see my years of hard work slipping away from me gradually, and my fingers had no strength to hold onto it.

I grew desperate for a solution, so I started attending Alcoholics Anonymous meetings two towns over. I figured that I could maintain some of my own anonymity that way; it just wouldn't do to have my own town talking about how low I'd gone. That was silly, of course, as gossip had started making its buzz long before this. But I never heard about any of it until much later on.

It was at the AA meetings that I met Trina. She had a similar circumstance. Her marriage ended in divorce, and she sought bottled numbness to get through the pain. As we poured out our lives to each other over coffee after one of the meetings, I felt a warm, growing connection to her. She openly admitted that she was feeling the same way. I used to snort at the concept of love at first sight, always figured it had more to do with hormones than anything else. But I wasn't so sure now. Despite a small voice of caution buzzing its one-note deep within my mind, I asked Trina to move in with me. She agreed.

A week later, we married.

I was back in a state of euphoria. I cut back on my drinking and plowed into work with an energy and exuberance I hadn't had for years. My financial situation stabilized. The company began to grow again. Trina and I had a perfect relationship.

For about a year.

It all started to change when she told me she was pregnant. At first I was chagrined to hear the news. I felt, at 46, I was too old to be having a newborn baby around the house. I tried to convince Trina that an abortion was the only answer, but she was adamantly opposed to the idea. This caused an ongoing low-level tension between us that cooled our relationship substantially. I grew frustrated at Trina's stubbornness, her unwillingness to consider the options. After all, she had children from her first marriage, and she was actually two years older than I. There was nothing beneficial about being the parent of a teenager when we were in our sixties, in my opinion.

I started nursing anger to resentment. We were supposed to be a team. We were supposed to be mature adults who could work together to solve our problems. Instead, she selfishly hung on to some sort of pregnancy-and-new-life-is-my-fountain-of-youth attitude. At least that's how I interpreted her defiant stance.

I began hitting the bar again after work. Many nights, I didn't get home until after 11:00 and Trina had already gone to bed by herself. It it seemed like I was growing more powerless each day to direct my life in the way I imagined it would be by now. I was seriously contemplating divorce, but feared the financial consequences of doing so.

And I feared being alone again.

I stumbled home around midnight after a particularly lugubrious session at the bar. My head was spinning, my stomach teetering on the edge of rebellion. The warm glow of rum had been replaced by fits of shivering. My mouth tasted like muddy water running through a garbage-filled gutter. I was miserable.

I went into the bedroom and climbed into bed without even taking my clothes off. I must have passed out immediately, because the next thing I knew Trina was shaking me vigorously. She was shouting my name, rather loudly.

Cocking open an eye, I looked at the clock. It said 2:47.

"Wha?" I mumbled.

Trina nearly shrieked, "My water broke! I'm having contractions!"

"Wha?" was all I could manage again. I tried to turn over on my side, but the bed suddenly felt like some sort of fun house slide and I was about to roll off it.

"Get up, James! You need to take me to the hospital." Trina was up and getting dressed. She turned on the overhead light. It shot laser beams of pain through my eyes and into my skull. Then nausea shot straight up from my bowels to the back of my throat. It was all I could do to keep from throwing up in the bed.

Trina stopped dressing long enough to stare at me hard.

"Oh God, you're still drunk," she finally said, resignedly.

I had no reply for that. She was right.

I tried laboriously to swing myself out of bed. I was already dressed and would take her to the hospital if it killed me. Then I found myself face down on the floor with a mouthful of carpet. I must have blacked out, for when I came around I was still lying there.

The phone by the bed was ringing loudly. It echoed in my seemingly empty brain chamber. I felt sick and wasted, but I could move a bit better now. I crawled up onto the bed and picked up the phone.

"Hello?"

"Mr. D'Angelo?" the caller asked.

"Yeah, that's me," I replied groggily.

"Mr. D'Angelo, this is the Essex County Sheriff's dispatch. We've been trying to get in touch with you. There has been an accident involving your wife on Interstate 76. You need to go to the Parkview Memorial Hospital immediately."

I looked at the clock. It said 5:56.

My head was swimming through a torrent of rancid honey which oozed in every direction. I thanked the caller. Then I threw up on the bedroom floor.

"Aw geeez, Trina's gonna kill me for that," I muttered to myself.

The odor of the vomit kept my stomach roiling, so I went downstairs to use the phone in the kitchen. Someone had replaced the hard flooring tiles with a soft, spongy rubber. Holding onto the counter I managed to grab the phone and plop onto a chair at the table.

I called the hospital, and after a series of transfers was able to talk with someone who was knowledgeable about the situation.

"Mr. D'Angelo, yes, we have Trina here. You should come in right away."

"I don't think that's possible. I'm very sick right now with the flu. Is she doing all right?" I asked.

"No, Mr. D'Angelo… neither she, nor the baby survived the crash."

The days that followed that night were mostly unmemorable. They were a robotic, swirling haze of activity, arrangements, and visitations. Friends and family contacted me with condolences, little realizing that I was mostly responsible for the death of my wife and unborn son. They had to suspect, however, especially as the story made the newspapers and evening local television news. Nothing was ever mentioned about my being drunk – they all reiterated the flu excuse I used when speaking to the hospital. But those who knew me had to know.

I was aching numb, hollow and devoid of any sensible thought. Tugs of guilt clawed at the edges of my being, and I knew it wouldn't be long before I was awash in it. I started keeping my .38 caliber revolver on the kitchen table in plain sight as I toyed with the idea of eating its muzzle for lunch one day.

I lost all interest in my insurance company and left it to my assistant to run until my leave of absence was over. It could fold and go defunct for all I cared at the moment, but others depended on it for their livelihoods.

Though this was the darkest moment of my life, I didn't feel like drinking. Perhaps I thought I didn't deserve the temporary oblivion it could provide from the pain. Perhaps I learned a horrible, yet effective lesson from the experience. Neither supposition mattered; just the thought of drinking made me feel ill, and that was sufficient.

Two weeks after Trina's funeral I received an unexpected phone call. As I mechanically answered it, I recognized a familiar voice at the other end.

"Aunt Ruth?? Hey, how are you? It's been a while, hasn't it?"

"Yes, Jimmy, a long time. Too long maybe. Your Uncle Leo has been asking for you."

"I'd really like to talk to him. Put him on, please."

"Not on the phone, Jimmy. Here, in person."

Something in her voice raised the hair on the back of my neck.

"What's wrong, Aunt Ruth?"

"Leo's dying, Jimmy. Of cancer." She sounded tired.

I felt a portion of my mind tilt crazily to one side and back again. My stomach dropped about six inches with a thud, and I had a strange urge to urinate.

"Damn." It was all I could think of to say. I paused for close to an eternity trying to organize my thoughts.

"Aunt Ruth?" I finally said.

"Yes Jimmy?"

"When should I come over?"

"This evening will be fine."

It was about a three hour drive to their house. All I could think during the entire drive was "First it was Trina, now it's Uncle Leo." I was in turmoil of agitation. In retrospect, I suddenly realized that they hadn't shown up at Trina's funeral. Now I knew why, and it was staggering my psyche, like a punch drunk boxer on his last legs.

I arrived at their house a little after 6:00 PM. Aunt Ruth answered the door. She was haggard and worn. I hugged her and was shocked at how bony she felt.

"This must be taking a lot out of you Aunt Ruth," I finally said.

"It's been difficult, Jimmy. Go on into the bedroom. Leo's waiting for you. I'll bring along some coffee in a bit." She smiled slightly and withdrew to the kitchen.

I went into the bedroom. It was fairly dark in there with only a small table lamp illuminating the area around the bed. Uncle Leo was lying still, and, at first, I thought he might be dead. It gave me a start when he stirred and opened his eyes. His face was flushed red with apparent pain.

"Uncle Leo." I almost whispered it. He didn't seem to hear me.

"Uncle Leo." I said it a little louder this time.

Without looking at me, he croaked out, "Jimmy? That you? Come here boy, next to the bed where I can see you better."

I grabbed a chair against the wall and moved it to the side of the bed where the light was shining. Sitting in the chair, I looked over his face. It was deeply lined, more so than I remembered it being when I saw him last. His arms were scrawny thin, more like dead tree branches than strong, vital limbs on a healthy body.

His nose was as pronounced as ever, and I wondered if it had gotten even larger over the years. His eyes were sharp, though, focused and unfogged in spite of the demon within him. Even more than clarity, his eyes reflected a fullness of wisdom that was both comforting and daunting at the same time.

"How are you doing Uncle Leo?" I asked meekly.

"I've done better Jimmy. I've also done worse." He went into a coughing spasm for a few seconds and then apologized for it.

"Aunt Ruth told me you've been asking for me, Uncle Leo," I said.

"Yeah, Ruthie, she's a good girl, Jimmy." He smiled. He was quiet for a little while.

I wondered if that was all he was going to say. Awkwardly, I reached out and took one of his hands. Despite the warm stuffiness of the room, it felt cold, much like the stones one would find deep in a cave.

"I'm sorry I haven't kept in touch, Uncle Leo. Things have been really hectic lately, and … and…"

"Shut up, Jimmy." His voice seemed stronger now.

"Yes, sir."

"A long time ago, when you was a kid, you wanted to know how my nose had saved my life. I told ya you wasn't ready at the time to hear it. You're ready now."

Confused, at first, I wasn't sure what he was talking about. Then the memories flooded back through me like a late night rerun.

"Ahh right." If my dying uncle wanted to tell me a story

about his nose, then who was I to argue? "Go right ahead, Uncle Leo. I'd love to hear it."

He looked at me and chuckled raspily, then coughed.

"You don't know what you're saying, Jimmy. But I've heard about you, and you're ready."

I gently set his hand onto the bed and sat back in my chair. I crossed my legs, folded my arms and prepared to hear what he had to say.

Uncle Leo took a sip from the water glass beside his bed. Then he began.

"I was a bit younger than you are now when two things happened. Life got real bad from circumstances beyond my control, and I started smelling funny things. Things I couldn't explain."

"What do you mean Uncle Leo?"

"Patience Jimmy, I'll get to it. I tried to do all kinds of things to fix my problems but none of them worked. I won't go into any of it, because that's not the point of the story. But suffice to say I was pretty low. Whiskey and me was best friends even though I suspected it was really tryin' to stick a knife in my back the whole time."

"I got disgusted with my life, and I got disgusted with me. I knew it was time to change something, but I didn't know what or how. Then one Sunday I was walking by a church. Its doors were open, and people were singing inside. I decided to go in." He paused to drink some more water.

Ohhh geez, Uncle Leo, I thought. Not a freaking church conversion story. I always knew Leo and Ruth were religious, but I managed to avoid any such discussions with them throughout my life. I figured it was fine for them; I just didn't see any advantage to going to church.

I didn't leave though. It seemed disrespectful to cut him short.

"I didn't stay."

"Huh?" I asked. That didn't sound right. "Did you say you didn't stay?"

"That's right. I walked into the church," he resumed. "They was singing some song I didn't know nothing about. I slipped into an empty pew in the back and picked up a hymnal to try and follow along. It all seemed a lot like the church my parents went to when I was young. But it was a strange song they sang. There was a lot of mention of sunshine and clouds and walking in the light of well-being. I just figured it was some sort of newfangled type of hymn, so I went along with it."

"Then my nose started picking up a strange whiff of something."

I sighed a little at this. "What was it Uncle Leo? Someone's perfume?"

"No. It wasn't so sweet as that. It was more like a rotten egg smell, but very faint. I just figured the person in the pew in front of me passed some wind or something...."

"Reminds me of an old joke," I interrupted.

Leo frowned at me and said, "I heard it before. Anyway, the singing got done and we sat down. The preacher gets up at the pulpit, only they don't call him a preacher at that church. They call him a Director. The Director gets up and starts talking about things that I don't recall ever hearing in a church before. I figure it's been a lot of years and maybe things are different now, so I stuck around some more."

"Then that smell came back. It was heavier this time, and I took to waving a sheet of paper in front of my face to try and wave it away. All the while the Director was talking about making dreams come true with positivity and some nicety type stuff."

"I'm thinking that the old gent in front of me, who kept yelling out "amen" ever' time the Director said something, had a plate full of beans for breakfast before church that morning and maybe I should find another place to sit. Funny thing is, no one else around us seemed to notice it. Maybe they was just too polite."

"The smell got real strong. Then it changed somehow. Instead of just being rotten egg, it started smelling like burnt metal or hot electrical wiring or something."

Leo's story was starting to interest me. Maybe this wasn't about religious things after all.

"I started getting a little nervous. I looked around to see if I could see smoke anywhere in the church, but I couldn't, not that it mattered. A fire can start in the walls and take a while to blow into full flame. But no one else acted like they smelled anything out of the ordinary. They just kept gaping at the Director like they was hypnotized. I decided to get out of that church before it burnt down around me and everyone else."

Uncle Leo stopped for a while to catch his breath. He was becoming a bit more animated while telling his story, and I feared that maybe it would tire him too much. When I stated my concern, he simply laughed and said he was dying anyway, so what was getting too tired?

"Is that what saved your life Uncle Leo? Getting out of the building in time?" I asked when he was breathing normally.

"Yes," he replied. "And no."

"What?"

"It wasn't a fire I smelled, Jimmy. That church is still standing today, still the same as it was back then only in worse shape from age. There was no fire then, hasn't been since."

"Well, then what was it?" I asked.

"I don't know exactly Jimmy. That ain't the end of the story though. I decided to try a different church the next Sunday, you know, the one two blocks over from here? The one with the nice fountain out front and the pretty gardens around the sides. I was there earlier than the start of the service, so I could get a good seat about halfway down. Turns out I didn't need to be there so early; there wasn't many people there."

"Let me guess Uncle Leo, you smelled egg salad at this church, too?"

"No, no, just wait a minute, eh? This is a normal church, has a minister and uses the old hymns that I used to know. The minister dresses in robes, looks like a Catholic priest, but he don't say nothing about butterflies or wishes or anything like that. We did our singing, they took our money and the minister gets up front to talk. Soon he's droning on about something to do with David and Saul, or maybe it was Moses and Aaron – I don't really recall. I started looking around at the people there. They looked like respectable enough folks, mostly old. They weren't real friendly, but I wasn't looking to make friends yet." He paused, sipped some water. "Then I smelled something again"

"What was it this time?"

"Do you remember, Jimmy, when the raccoon died under our house?"

I nodded. It happened when I was about 10, but the memory of it was vivid.

"Do you remember the horrible smell that kicked up from it? It was in the middle of summer, hot, and that carcass was decaying in a place that was near impossible to get at. Well, that's what I smelled at this church. It got so strong, I 'bout near gagged in the middle of the service. But I held out until the end. It smelled like a rotting corpse, like an open tomb."

"Did you ask anyone about the odor, Uncle Leo?"

"Nah, I just hightailed it out. There was a small group of women standing near the door gossiping about someone in the neighborhood, and the smell was strongest when I passed them. Thought maybe one of them old girls had best get home and clean herself up. But there was no smell when I went out the door, and no one in that church had the slightest nose twitch."

I was leaning forward now. This was a strange story Leo was telling me. These odors in church – maybe they were psychosomatic. Maybe he imagined them because he was in places he didn't really want to be. I'm no psychologist, and I don't know if that is possible. But I couldn't think of any other reason for it all.

I told Uncle Leo about my theory. He looked at me with his wise, old eyes. They seemed a little sad in a way. He nodded and went on.

"I thought something like that, too, Jimmy. I don't think that anymore, though."

"Why is that, Uncle Leo?"

"Because I decided to try one more church. I figured if it smelled too, then I was either allergic to churches, or churchgoing just wasn't my destiny. So the next Sunday, I chose a little church just outside the city limits. In fact, it's out in the country a bit, sitting in that field where the fishing creek runs through."

The mention of the fishing creek made me smile. Some of my fondest childhood memories revolved around going fishing in that creek with Uncle Leo. My dad died when I was five, so I never got to do much with him. Uncle Leo became sort of a surrogate father to me.

"I think I remember that church. It was a pretty small chapel type place, wasn't it?"

"A long time ago, yep. It's larger now, but still pretty in a country way." Leo's voice was starting to get really raspy, and his breathing was labored. "The folks I met were wonderful, and the service was beautiful. Then I met him."

"Him who, Uncle Leo?" I asked.

Leo turned to look at me with eyes that burned like fiery coals. He took a deep breath which made him cough roughly.

Then he said, "Him – Jesus Christ. I became a follower of the Lord Jesus Christ that day Jimmy. He saved me from eternal damnation, and when I die, I will see Him face to face." Leo sighed and fell silent.

"That's it, Uncle Leo?" I was perplexed, and a little miffed. It seemed that Uncle Leo had concocted an entire story just to tell me about his religious conversion. I had to keep reminding myself that this was an old man on his deathbed, that I should be patient and compassionate.

"No Jimmy, that's not it. Not it at all," he finally whispered. A tear started seeping down his cheek. "He didn't only save me from Hell in the afterlife, but he helped me out of the hell I was in in this life. With his strength, I kicked my alcoholism. Ruthie and I got along better – we was close to divorce, dontcha know. It hasn't been all daisies, life still gives you problems. But when I rely upon him, the problems seem to work themselves out sooner, or they are at least more tolerable."

"But Uncle Leo, what about your nose, what about the odors you kept smelling? Did you smell anything at this church?" I was afraid he'd lost the thread of the story.

Leo smiled, his eyelids half closed. He looked as if he was going to sleep. Or perhaps something else.

"Yes Jimmy. When I went into that church the first time," he was still whispering. "I smelled the most wonderful smell."

I leaned closer; his voice was starting fade out. "What was it, Uncle Leo?"

"Uncle Leo?"

"Uncle Leo?"

He stirred a little. He looked straight up toward the ceiling, a far-away distance in his eyes.

Finally he said, "Jimmy. It smelled like freshly baked bread."

When I left Uncle Leo's room, he was sleeping. There was a smile on his face as if his dreams were peaceful, not pain-wracked. I said goodbye to Aunt Ruth and drove home the three hours with my head buzzing by Uncle Leo's story, but my heart very heavy with sorrow heaped upon sorrow. It was as if I was peering down a long corridor with the lights off and I had no idea where its end was.

I slept fitfully that night. I dreamed that Trina, Uncle Leo and a little boy were on a boat that was slowly sinking out in the middle of a large lake. They didn't seem to notice, but they kept waving and smiling at me as I stood on the shore and watched. Just as the boat slipped under the surface, I bolted awake from the phone ringing beside the bed.

I stared at it for a second. I knew what it was, why it was ringing.

Finally I picked it up. "Hello, Aunt Ruth."

"Jimmy, your Uncle Leo passed on just twenty minutes ago." There was a gasp of breath, a sob, and the phone went dead.

"I know, Aunt Ruth," I whispered into the phone. "I know."

I attended Uncle Leo's funeral with a firm plan in mind as to what I would do afterwards. In many ways, I felt calmer than I had in a long time. The gnawing senses of loneliness and guilt had quieted with my decision, allowing me the full force of mourning. Once again, Uncle Leo played surrogate as I grieved over both him and Trina at his funeral. I wept unabashedly when I saw him lying in his casket.

After the funeral, Aunt Ruth pulled me aside, asked me if I would come by her house for refreshments. I smiled and gave her a long hug.

"I'm sorry, Aunt Ruth, but I have to run," I said.

"Do you really, Jimmy?" she asked.

"Yes, Aunt Ruth. Life comes in threes, don't you know?" I said, rather lightly.

Concern spread over her face. "I'll be praying for you, Jimmy."

"Thank you, Aunt Ruth," I replied. With that I walked into the darkness.

I drove out of the town, out into the country a bit, to the field where the fishing creek ran through. I had my .38 revolver sitting on the passenger's seat beside me, not caring if anyone saw it or not. Uncle Leo's church was brightly lit as a beacon on a dark, craggy shore.

I took care to park the car at the far end of the church's parking lot away from the other vehicles there. Then I picked up the gun and got out. I decided to leave the keys in the ignition as I wouldn't need them any more.

I walked through the field to where the creek babbled noisily. I stood for a moment, just listening. I remembered the carefree days of childhood, fishing for little trout in that creek with Uncle Leo. I thought about Mandy, my first wife, and felt a great veil of shame fall over me for how I treated her, Jim Jr. and Sandy, my two kids. I spoke to the sky, asking them to forgive me. I thought about Trina and our unborn baby son and pleaded their forgiveness, too.

Then I put the barrel of the revolver in my mouth.

Before I could pull the trigger, I smelled a pleasing aroma. It washed over me like a clean breath of wind. It smelled like a field of flowers on a late Spring day. It smelled like newly mown grass in mid-Summer when the sun is going down.

But mostly, it smelled like freshly baked bread.

I heard Uncle Leo whisper, "Then I met him. Jesus Christ."

I pulled the gun from my mouth, stared at its steely glint in the moonlight. It looked evil.

Throwing it to the ground, I started walking towards the lights of the church.

WAITING FOR SHERRIE
(2008)

Mark's face froze as he stared at the image on his computer monitor. He glanced around quickly, almost guiltily, to see if anyone was observing him. It was unnecessary. He was the only one in the office at the moment.

Looking back at the monitor, Mark allowed himself a slight smile. It had been years since he'd seen her. A lot of years. The last time they spoke on the phone, he informed her that he was getting married. She seemed put off by the news, silent for a while at first, then softly saying, "Well, that's a big decision. Are you sure you're ready?"

Mark had chuckled inwardly at that. That was so like her – always questioning his decisions. During the time they dated, she had a tendency to take control of things while Mark was always pretty easy-going. Over time it started to grate on him, but that wasn't the cause of the break up.

Sherrie and Mark had been dating exclusively through the school year. On Thanksgiving break he went home with her and met her parents. They were wonderfully nice folks who accepted him as if they'd been friends for years. During winter break, Sherrie went home with Mark to meet his parents. They took Mark aside during the visit and commented how much they liked Sherrie over all his past girlfriends.

Their future seemed set in stone.

They talked of marriage, made tentative plans as to how to work it all out with the remainder of their school time. They even discussed about when to start having children.

Then it happened.

Mark had walked to the apartment Sherrie was sharing with three other classmates. She met him on the front porch.

With no hesitation, Sherrie said, "Mark, I don't want to see you as much any more."

Mark was stunned. His heart dropped down into his shoes, and his brain puffed into hot cotton.

All he could manage was, "Huh?"

Sherrie repeated, "I don't want to see you as much any more."

Mark seemed to stutter for days before he blurted out, "Why??? What does that mean??"

Quietly, she said, "I'm not ready for a serious relationship. I want to see other people."

"So… how often, ahh, when do I… um. What do you mean not as much any more!!!??" he nearly screamed, desperately trying to control his emotions.

Sherrie looked away, "I don't know what it means. We'll have to figure it out as we go."

Mark looked wildly about as if hoping to see Candid Camera jumping out from behind the nearby rhododendron bush.

"But, but, but… "

"I have to go Mark. You can call me at the end of the week if you want. We'll talk then." Sherrie turned and went back inside the house.

Mark watched the door close. His hands opened and clenched without his realizing it. He stared at the door for about five minutes before he turned away and walked back to his dorm room. The next few days were a blur. There was a persistent feeling of lead weight in Mark's stomach. At times he sensed a blind panic threatening to overtake him.

Mark felt like a train derailed. He'd gone through breakups before. But there had always been signs; it was easier to prepare. Sherrie had left no signs, or at least anything Mark could recognize as such.

They had just returned from her parents' home in Virginia the week before. It was their second trip south. Everything was terrific. Mark helped Sherrie's dad with a home project; impressed him with his ability to work with wood. He felt more like a member of the family than ever before. Sherrie chatted almost nonstop about marriage, children and careers on the very long drive back to the school.

In the following week they studied together several times, ate out a couple times, and went into the city Saturday to catch a movie and take a walk through the Public Garden.

Then on Monday afternoon, Sherrie lowered her swift, sharp hatchet onto Mark's head and split him right down the middle. When Friday came about, Mark wasn't sure whether he should call her or not. He finally decided he would – he missed her terribly – and as he went to the payphone in the hall, he had an odd sensation that invisible strings were moving his arms, hands and feet.

His heart started fluttering. His breath came in short spurts. Mark was nervous as he dialed her number. What should he say? How should he sound? Delighted? Affectionate? Angry?

Each ring jangled his mind, laid down new blocks of fear in his growing wall.

"Hello?"

Mark blew a gush of air at the wall. It was Joy, one of Sherrie's roommates.

"Ah, hi Joy. How are you?" He said with some relief..

"Mark! I'd like to ask you the same thing. How are YOU?"

"Hey, I'm doing OK, Joy," he stated with forced cheerfulness. "Actually, I'm not doing so good."

"I wouldn't think so. Sherrie told me what was going on. I'm sorry to hear it, Mark. I don't know what's wrong with her. All she will say is that she has to think about her life from now on, whatever that means. I asked 'what about Mark's life?' but she didn't answer."

Mark smiled at that. "Thank you, Joy. You're a good friend. Would... would Sherrie be there... by any chance?"

"No, she went out with Jackie and Diane. Should I have her call you when she gets back?"

Mark thought about this for a long moment. "No, Joy. Thanks anyway. I'll try another time...... g'bye."

"Bye Mark, call me any time you need to talk. OK?"

"Thanks, Joy. I might do that." Mark hung up.

He went back to his room, turned off the light and sat in the dark until his roommate returned a few hours later. Sherrie apparently had not remembered (or cared) that Mark was supposed to call her. She was carving out a new life and he was simply a dangling remnant of the old. How quickly it all changed.

The school year ended, summer started. Mark remained in the mostly empty dorm while Sherrie stayed in her apartment. He worked nights as a security guard in a large department store in the city. She worked days on campus.

Mark tried to see Sherrie on whatever capricious schedule she made for them. It was made even more difficult by their work schedules.

In the morning when he returned from work, he would stand in the stairwell of the dorm and look out the window that faced the married students' apartment building. Now and then, he could see her in the lobby vacuuming or cleaning the glass doors. He would place his hand against the window as if trying to reach her. Then he would shake his head sadly, go back to his room and go to bed.

He hoped that her decision would be a short term bit of craziness from which she would eventually shake free. But she was usually aloof to the point of being uncaring. Mark had become more of an afterthought to Sherrie than anything else. Even so, she wouldn't end the relationship totally.

Come mid-summer, Mark couldn't stand it any more. He made a decision to stop trying to see Sherrie at all. School would be starting again in about 40 days and he needed to move on. He wouldn't call her, take her out or even gaze at her through distant windows. It was an act of survival.

At first, it was difficult. His desire to see Sherrie tugged at Mark physically. He started drinking to try to escape the prevalent pain that dogged his waking hours. It didn't really help; in fact, it made him more depressed. When one of the other guards at work passed a joint around, Mark tried it. In fact, he tried several dubious things just to gain a temporary breath of relief. Each new thrill, though, crashed when a certain song played on the radio, when a certain cologne wafted past him.

The cure finally came with time.

A sense of normalcy, balance re-established itself by late August. Mark told his roommate that he felt as if he'd been swimming underwater the whole summer and just came up for air. He looked forward to the start of school in a couple weeks, regrouping with returning friends and generally moving on. He was sure he'd see Sherrie around campus, and it would be uncomfortable for a while.

Of course, Mark never dreamed that they would be in the same Physiological Psychology class. He never could have imagined that the professor would pair them up to do research into the physiology of sexual response.

It was an awkward moment, approaching the professor. On a small campus, however, news usually gets around fast. The professor allowed him to pair up with another class member with a different topic. Sherrie had to go it alone. Mark saw a pleasant irony in that.

The school year passed. Everything went well, for the most part - typical school year. Mark dated Brenda, a professor's daughter, for most of the year. She broke his heart at the end as well, but it wasn't as devastating as the breakup with Sherrie.

Then, in a bizarre twist, Sherrie asked Mark to take her to the Junior-Senior Formal Banquet. Even more surprising to Mark was that he agreed.

He enjoyed the evening. Sherrie was pleasant and warm. Mark felt some of the old excitement noodling at the edges of his spirit. After the banquet, when she suggested they drive down to the beach to watch the moon-silvered waves, he was hooked.

They started dating again as if the previous summer had never happened. Mark was pleased, but guarded. He wasn't going to allow himself to go into this blindly. If Sherrie wanted to deepen the relationship and move toward something more committed, then he might just allow it. Otherwise, he was calling the shots.

After a couple months of bliss, Mark went to her apartment for a visit. When she answered the door, she saw Mark and said, "What are you doing here?"

The tone of her voice was not one of warm welcome.

Mark was taken aback by the question, but managed to maintain a calm demeanor. He nodded knowingly.

"Nothing, I guess. See ya, Sherrie." Then he turned and walked back to the campus. Even with his carefully constructed self-defense, her question still stung him. He wasn't sure what she wanted or why she wanted whatever it was. Mark had no contact with her for the next six months. She never called him.

When he finally ran into her, she asked where he had been. Mark was cagey. He figured he didn't owe her anything, so he just laughed and said he'd been busy. This would be the last time he would see her while at school.

It was Mark's senior year. He was scrambling to figure out what to do after graduation. He was sure he wasn't going on to grad school, and an education in Psychology didn't particularly lend itself well to a career path without higher degrees. When his friend, Glen, told him he was joining the Army, Mark was incredulous. Anti-establishment Glen was going to become a part of the establishment after all.

When Glen suggested he talk to a recruiter, Mark snickered. But as Glen described the bonuses and benefits of enlistment, he became intrigued. It appealed to his sense of adventure, a hunger for something different and his desire to get his college loans paid off quickly. Plus it would totally go against anything Sherrie would ever expect of him.

So he did it.

Basic training was at Fort Dix, New Jersey. As he jumped from foxhole to foxhole, throwing grenades and firing his weapon, Mark would wonder what Sherrie would think if she could see him. As he ran for miles in formation, yelling out cadence, Mark would imagine Sherrie watching him from the sidewalk, and he'd get an energetic thrill. As he limped in from the twenty-mile road march, all Mark could think about was sitting down for a long time.

Advanced individual training was at Fort Devens, Massachusetts. Here the Army was more about learning your job than it was about combat practices and skills. There was a college feel to its campus, but Mark never mistook it for anything other than another Army post. Physical training, inspections and field exercises remained standard protocol. Still it was easier than basic training, and Mark strongly considered making the Army a career. By this time, his memories of Sherrie were dissolving into the background – especially since the barracks were co-ed.

After Fort Devens, Mark received his permanent duty assignment. He was to be stationed at Fort Stewart, Georgia. The deep south. He'd never been there before, and he was filled with a mixed dose of curiosity and trepidation. The trepidation was partly due to location, but also due to the fact that this was a tactical assignment when he would have preferred a strategic one.

At a strategic post, Mark would have worked a daily job in a field station, most likely in a foreign country. At Fort Stewart, however, there was bound to be a lot of field exercises, weapons training, inspections, physical training – in other words, basic training all over again. This time, however, it would be for years instead of weeks.

That's exactly what it turned out to be ... almost like basic training. But there was nothing Mark could do about it, so he made the best of the situation. There were exercises in the swamps around the post, in the Mojave Desert in California. There were room inspections, equipment inspections, personal inspections. Every morning, everyone was up at 6:00 doing pushups, situps, and other exercises capped off with a two-mile (or more) run.

There were interminable hours in the motor pool PMCSing the team vehicles. Mark knew none of this would be permanent; that it would all come to an end one day. In the meantime, he just had to endure and dream of the day he could leave the post as a civilian.

In the middle of all the mundanity, Mark received word that he had a phone call in the orderly room.

"That's odd," he thought. "Must be my parents – maybe bad news?"

He arrived in the orderly room and picked up the phone the CQ had left sitting on the desk.

"Hello? Specialist Plummer speaking."

"Hi Mark!" The voice on the other end was light and airy. It was musical champagne, effervescent and velvet.

Mark gulped. "Sherrie??"

A light laugh. Mark could feel his heart quiver.

"Probably didn't expect to hear from me again, did you?" Sherrie said demurely.

"N-no, but it's wonderful hearing your voice! How did you find out where I was?"

"I called your parents, Mark. Listen, I have to come down to Savannah on business next week. Would you like to get together?"

Mark felt his face flush.

"Wow, yeah! I'd love to. When will you be here?"

She told him. They made plans to meet at her hotel.

When Mark hung up the phone, he was in a happy daze. He couldn't explain it; he thought he'd left her far behind. There wouldn't (couldn't) be any expectations this time around. They were just going to get together for a very short time and then move on with their lives. Still, he knew he had an idiotic smile on his face as he walked back to the barracks.

The days until the date dragged as anticipation grew.

When the day finally came, Mark nearly ran back to his barracks room after final formation. He showered and changed into civilian clothes – nothing too nice, just cool casual. The 40-mile drive to Savannah took about three days it seemed. It was difficult to separate nerves from anticipation, so Mark quit trying. Then he was at her hotel.

There was no mistaking it – it was very good to see Sherrie again. Her hair was a little shorter and she had looked as trim as when he first started dating her three years ago. She was warm, even affectionate.

They went to dinner on River Street. A delightful seafood dinner followed the appetizer of raw oysters on the half shell. Jazzy music was playing in the background. The atmosphere was embracing without being suffocating. Afterwards, they strolled along the riverwalk and talked. The sultry evening air was as intoxicating as liquor. Mark found himself babbling on and on about Army life. Sherrie listened intently. As they sat on a park bench which overlooked the Savannah River, he felt Sherrie slip her arm into his and snuggle close. Something like love, but a little cooler, flooded through Mark, both relaxing and exhilarating him. It also alarmed him somewhat. This was not something he had envisioned. A get together as friends who were once very intimate (he felt like he knew her better than any other person), some dinner, a chat and handshake – that's what he thought would happen.

Instead, they went back to her hotel room, and Mark didn't leave until 1:30 the next morning. He returned to Fort

Stewart knowing that his night of abbreviated sleep would leave him sapped come daylight. But it had been worthwhile on some level being with her again. It had revealed to him that the years had hardened him to her, that he didn't really love her anymore. At least not in the naïve, innocent way he did originally. He thought he might be able to carry on an affair with her for as long as she wanted and not be the worse for it when she decided she didn't.

Things didn't work out quite that way.

It was difficult to keep something alive with Sherrie living two states away. They kept in touch sporadically by phone, she usually calling him. The last time they spoke, Mark called her to tell her the news of his impending marriage to a lovely southern lady named Marissa. That's when she replied, "Well, that's a big decision. Are you sure you're ready?"

Mark wanted to know if he hurt Sherrie with the news at all the same way she had hurt him in the past. But he found that his thirst for vengeance had mostly dissipated since meeting Marissa.

He simply answered, "Yeah, I'm ready."

She wished him well. They said goodbye.

Mark felt an odd hollowness as he hung up the phone.

That was twenty-two years ago.

Surfing across Sherrie's webpage brought it all flooding back through Mark's memory as if it had just happened.

It was no accident.

Mark had been searching for her much like he searched for many people from his past. The internet had been a great source of reunions with old friends. Mark especially enjoyed the surprise value of sending an email from "out of the blue" to someone he hadn't spoken with for over two decades.

He wasn't seeking to reconnect with Sherrie. He loved Marissa, loved being married to her. Rekindling an old romance was out of the question. But there was curiosity, and prior searches over the years had led nowhere.

Mark stared at the screen. Her face peered back at him with a soft half-smile that used to drive him crazy. She had aged; it was obvious from the photo. Her face was a bit fuller. There were small lines around her eyes that hadn't been there when he saw her last. A few small streaks of gray peaked out from her brown, flowing hair. This surprised Mark as she was particular about how her hair looked. But Sherrie still looked so much like the woman he once loved that he couldn't move his eyes from the monitor screen.

"Who's that?"

Mark jumped. "Wha?! Geez Dan, I almost had a heart attack!!" he said swiveling around in his chair. He looked at Dan who had a grin on his face.

"So, who is that you're looking at?"

Mark glanced over his shoulder at the computer screen. "She's someone I knew a long time ago... an old friend."

Dan laughed. "Yeah, right. A friend, eh? Do you always stare at old friends like that?"

"How long have you been watching me?"

"Long enough to know you are using the internet at work for personal purposes."

"Oh c'mon Dan! I've seen you on eBay and Amazon many times. Besides, I'm still on my lunch hour."

"I'm not warning you or anything, just making an observation, hmmmm." Dan sauntered back to his cubicle on the other side of the office.

Mark shook his head and turned back to his computer. His email alert was flashing.

Clicking on the icon, the email program sprang to full size. In bold, at the top of his email list was a message from *sdh59@freemail.com*. The subject line simply said, "Hi there!"

"Probably spam," Mark muttered. He opened it anyway just to make sure before entering the email address into the spam filter. This is what the message said,

Hi there,

I noticed you visited my site on oldfriendsreunited.com. Is this Mark Plummer from Quincy, Massachusetts? If so, it's really good to see you again. Feel free to drop me an email and we'll chat.☺

Mark read the email with growing disbelief. When he saw the signature, a chill went up the back of his neck.

Regards,
Sherrie Gammon

Mark blinked. He blinked again. Sherrie!

People were starting to drift back into the office. Lunch hour was drawing to an end. Quickly, he forwarded the email to his online account and shut down his internet browser. Letting out a long breath, he reached for the stack of paperwork in the in-box to his right and began shuffling through it.

Sherrie!

A flood of questions poured through his mind. Is it THE Sherrie? It had to be, that was her name, and Mark was at her page on that website. But how did she know? That didn't matter, really, did it? Should he email her? Why not? They are, after all, old friends, aren't they? What would Marissa think? Lord knows, he didn't want to hurt her or make her uncomfortable. What if an old boyfriend of Marissa's tried to contact her? That would be OK, wouldn't it? Just old friends, right?

Sherrie!

She seemed so historical, so much in the past. Of course, she'd still be in the present somewhere, but their circles spun far apart from each other. Maybe Mark would just send an email to say hi, to catch up a bit. Something friendly and pleasant. That wouldn't cause any problems. Sherrie was probably married, so everything would have to be above board. If he just kept it as email, then Marissa wouldn't have to know anyway. Yes! That would be best.

Wow! Sherrie.

Mark marveled at how calm he was. He realized that people did this sort of thing all the time, but there had to be some excitement or anticipation. He would have to tell her all about Marissa and the girls; let her know that he was a dedicated family man. She would tell him about her husband and kids. Everything would be cordial, platonic.

But the memories, the history - Mark could still feel the pain from that first breakup every time he closed his eyes and visualized it. How does one ignore everything that had taken place back then when it shaped his life the way it did? He had always felt like there was unfinished business between the two of them. Unfortunately, Mark had no idea how to finish it, or what was even required to put it all to rest.

He grew angry with himself. None of this should matter. None of it. He had Marissa now. She was a wonderful mate and mother. If he had to go back in time to consider the decision to marry her again, he'd do it with no second thoughts.

Even as his anger subsided, a new realization came to him. Sherrie was a part of him that Marissa could never expunge. His preference and love for Marissa could not change the fact that Sherrie was a very important, vital piece of his history, his development of who he was today. Marissa was also a part of him as well. If the future ever saw to it that he would end up alone only to meet a new love, she would never be able to replace what Marissa had meant to him. It wasn't about competition at all.

It was just a part of normal life experience. Wasn't it?

That night, just before going to bed, Mark logged into his online email account. "Hi there", as bold and brazen as before, tempted him like a crisp, new one hundred dollar bill. He opened the email, saw Sherrie's name at the bottom and fired off a quick reply. Then he went to bed.

As Mark crawled under the covers, Marissa snuggled next to him and sleepily murmured, "Whatcha been up to?"

Mark kissed her on the forehead and whispered, "Just sending off a quick email to someone who asked me a question today. Love ya." He turned onto his side and let Marissa spoon him. She whispered, "Love you, too." and was soon breathing softly, regularly.

Mark sighed. It was a long time before he fell asleep.

The next day Mark was at work when the email came in. The company where he worked had fairly strict personal email policies during work hours, but Mark decided to read it anyway. When he finished, he gulped.

Sherrie was coming!

Mark forwarded the message to his online email address and deleted it from his inbox. Sitting back in his chair, he rubbed his eyes until they burned.

Sherrie was coming. She was going to be in the area on business. She was proposing a meeting.

This is what her message said:

Hi Mark!

How delightful to find you again after all these years. I'm so glad you responded to my email. If you are still living in the greater Boston area, I'd like to get together with you for dinner some day next week. I will be in Boston for training for the week. Bring your wife, if you'd like. It would be a pleasure to meet her. Email me when you get the chance, and we'll make plans.

Affectionately,
Sherrie ☺

Now what was he supposed to do with that? Swapping emails was one thing – maybe a bit covert, but harmless nonetheless. Meeting Sherrie was something totally different. An inner voice spoke to him:

"Oh come on, Mark! You're not looking to hook up with her again. So what's the big deal?"

No, he wasn't looking to start something again. He had Marissa. He was happy with Marissa. Sherrie was history. Ancient history.

"Yes, you love Marissa. It's not like you plan on trying to get Sherrie to go to bed with you. It's a dinner, some conversation and then goodbye, adios, buenos dias, arrivederci."

If he did go, should he bring his wife? It would be the reasonable thing to do, wouldn't it? And it would ensure that Marissa had no reason to fear losing him.

Losing him? That was a bit drastic.

It would simply show respect for Marissa. There, that's good. Respect.

"OK, what if the conversation goes into the past? Wouldn't that make it uncomfortable for Marissa? Maybe it'd be better if she wasn't there."

Wait a minute, Mark thought. His internal argument seemed to be implying that going to dinner with Sherrie was a foregone conclusion. But then, maybe it was. Maybe he really had no decision in this at all. Maybe he was no better than a puppet whose strings were being controlled by powers beyond his comprehension.

"Don't get overly dramatic, Markie boy. It's just a dinner.

Two old friends meeting to catch up on the years that have passed. Or is there something else...??"

Is there? Mark was taken aback by the question. He would have to think about that one. Snorting, he returned to the work at hand. There was time to make a decision. A rational decision. Yet he couldn't seem to focus on his work. Instead he kept trying to draft a reply to Sherrie – a reply that struck a good balance between interest and noninterest, eagerness and nonchalance.

There was time to make a decision, but in reality it had already been made.

When Mark returned home that evening, he found the note Marissa had left for him:

Hi Sweetie,

I've taken the girls shopping for school clothes. There is some leftover chicken and rice in the refrigerator. Should be back by 8:30.

Love You!
Marissa

Mark fingered the note, thinking about Marissa, Jessie and Erica. Both girls looked so much like their mom that he used to joke that they needed to have a boy so Mark could have his own reproduction. He adored his three ladies which made him wonder why he felt the need to see Sherrie once again.

Need. Yes, it went beyond simple desire.

Mark went to his computer. When it had booted, he logged into his email account and wrote:

Hi Sherrie,

I think it would be a great idea to get together and catch up with each other. Unfortunately, my wife is out of town all next week, so she won't be able to join us. Let me know the best day for dinner, and I'll put it in my schedule. I look forward to seeing you again – it's been a long time!

Yours,
Mark

He moved his mouse to click "Send" and paused for a minute. Staring hard at the message, he set his cursor and replaced "*Yours*" with "*Affectionately*". Was it a wise thing to do? Mark wasn't sure, but clicked "Send" anyway.

That night Mark dreamed he was looking for something he had lost, but was unable to find it.

The date was set. A few more emails refined the where and when of the meeting. Mark was to meet Sherrie in the lobby of the Boston Marriott Long Wharf at 5:00 PM. From there they would walk to Durgin Park in Quincy Market for dinner. That morning, as Mark showered and shaved for work, he hummed a lively tune he remembered from the 80s.

When he sat down for breakfast, Marissa said, "You must be in a good mood today."

"Huh? Why's that, honey?"

"It's not often you sing in the shower."

Mark's face flushed a little. "Oh, I wasn't singing. Just humming a song I heard the other day on the radio. Can't get it out of my head." He smiled.

Marissa smiled back. "Are you going to be able to get home early tonight? Erica has her flute recital at 7:00; we need to be there by 6:30."

Mark froze, the smile on his face remained as if etched in stone. Then he covered his face with one hand and groaned.

"Oh no, Mark. What's wrong?"

"Oh honey, I can't make it," he said, hoping he had the right amount of anguish in his voice.

Marissa was piqued. "Why not? We planned this for a long time."

Mark shook his head back and forth. "Our department scheduled a strategic meeting for tonight after work. It's supposed to go for a couple hours. I'm so sorry. I completely forgot about the recital."

"Well, can't you get out of it?" her voice rose.

"No, it's mandatory," he sighed.

"Erica's going to be hurt," said Marissa in a bargaining tone.

"I know. I know. And I'm really sorry. Look, I'll take her to the movies this weekend if that will help. I'll take all of us." Mark reached across the table and squeezed Marissa's hand. She didn't respond.

Marissa turned her head away, muttered, "Do what you feel you need to do."

Mark nodded, stood up. He spoke tersely.

"Please tell Erica I'm sorry. They only have these

meetings once a year. It's just a case of unfortunate scheduling."

Marissa started clearing the table. "Maybe you can call her tonight before your meeting and apologize yourself." That ended the conversation.

Mark drove to work with a heavy feeling of shame and some irritation. He made every effort to attend his daughters' functions, to cheer them on or be there for support if they didn't quite succeed. Marissa knew this, so he couldn't understand why she was so upset with him. It's not as if he recklessly and selfishly blew it off.

"Whoa, wait a minute. You aren't going to the recital because you are meeting with an old girlfriend!"

Oh.... right. But Marissa didn't know that. He had lied convincingly enough; he was sure of it.

"How can you be absolutely certain? How do you know that you aren't throwing away the life you built for the last twenty years?"

He had lied to Marissa. That bothered him more than he could've known it would. But how would she have taken it if he'd told her the truth? And how could he have explained just what this meeting meant to him?

"It means more than missing your daughter's recital?"

No! How could that be? Yet, he was still determined to see Sherrie again. He had to know something, something that nibbled at his ragged edges of being ever since the first breakup. It was something that only Sherrie could explain, for Mark had come up with no explanation for it all these years.

Back and forth it went all the way to work. As he entered the workplace, Mark put on his business face determined to plow through the day as quickly as possible. There was sufficient work to stay busy until around 3:30. After he placed the last report into a courier pouch, Mark returned to the website where he first saw Sherrie.

She still gazed at him with the half-smile unique to her. His mind drifted back over the years again as he replayed various scenes within his head. The dates, the times spent together not doing much of anything but being together, the make out sessions. They had seemed so one, so unified. Like pieces of a complex puzzle that fit together perfectly to create a special whole. Mark felt the same way with Marissa, just not as intensely. Maybe that feeling went away after being with one person for a long time. Maybe he had felt that way about Marissa early on; he couldn't really remember.

The saying 'familiarity breeds contempt' flashed through his head. He could understand it, but thought it also bred comfort and reliability. Intensity, however, somehow got lost in the shuffle of years.

4:30. It was time for Mark to leave. The hotel was five blocks away from his office. He was going to leave his car in the parking garage and walk there. It was a lovely evening out, not too warm, not too cool. It would stay light outside until about 8:00 at night. The sidewalks were well lit, so it wouldn't be a problem.

Mark took a deep breath as he started walking. There was an undefinable fragrance of sweetness in the air which surprised him. Usually the odor of car and truck exhaust prevailed in this part of the city so close to the central artery.

The blocks slipped by. With each step, Mark felt lighter, more energetic than he had in a long time. Excitement crept in from the deep wells of his spirit. It washed over him like a fine, cool fountain spray on a hot summer day. It had been a long journey. At the end of it was Sherrie.

There was a sidewalk vendor right before the hotel selling flowers. Without a thought, Mark stopped and bought a dozen roses.

"Why did you do that? You bought roses for someone you haven't seen for decades. When was the last time you bought roses for your wife?"

Mark looked at the roses in his hand and frowned. Why did he buy them? It seemed like such a logical action he didn't think anything of it. For that matter, why was he going to see Sherrie? She dumped him a long time ago. He moved on. She moved on. What about his family?

Mark started to grow nervous as he entered the hotel lobby. It wasn't the good, anticipatory nervousness he knew so well in the past. It was a sickly nervousness shaded with tinges of paranoia. He was going to see a woman who wasn't his wife. He'd lied to his wife in order to be able to do this. He could just turn around and walk out of the hotel room, then explain in an email about having a surprise department meeting he had to attend.

"What if someone sees you?"

That was the crux of it, wasn't it. Boston is a huge city. Most of the time, you never see anyone else you know outside of your workplace. The irony, however, is that when you do run into someone, it's when you least expect or want it.

Mark had to see this through. He had too much deceit invested in it to back out now. Looking around the lobby, he spied some chairs off to the side. He had the option of sitting to face the elevators or face the door. Not knowing from which direction Sherrie would come, Mark opted to face the elevators. That would leave his back to the door, but he could hear people going in and out.

He sat down and waited. It was 4:47. Thirteen minutes. Sherrie said she'd meet him at 5:00. It was a busy lobby. Mark watched the activity around him. People were checking in, getting on and off elevators, milling about looking at tourist brochures and reading newspapers.

Mark looked at his watch again. It was 5:00. Sherrie was punctual, so he expected her to show up any minute. One of the elevators was humming. He could see that it was coming down from an upper floor by the lights flashing over it. This must be her.

He started to rise, to walk over to the elevator. He gripped the roses tightly, crinkling the cellophane wrapper. His breathing was shallow, in short spurts. His heart was pounding.

Halfway to the elevators, the door opened. Mark stopped. Nothing happened at first, then someone came out.

It was an elderly couple. Mark closed his eyes, took a deep breath.

"Hello, Mark," a voice said behind him. That voice, so familiar! Mark's heart jumped. He whirled around and shouted,

"Kyle!"

Sitting in the chair beside the one he'd sat in was his brother-in-law, Kyle. Mark's face turned red. He felt desperate to not be there. Trying to gather himself together on the fly, he walked back to his chair and sat down.

"How long have you been here, Kyle?" he asked with a forced calmness.

"Oh I sat down just a few minutes before you stood up to go to the elevators. You must not have heard me," Kyle replied pleasantly.

Mark cast a glance over at the elevators. Another door was opening. A young professional woman and gentleman came out.

"So what brings you to the Marriott, man?" Mark asked looking at his wife's brother, a make believe smile on his face.

"I was going to ask you the same question, Mark."

"Oh, I just have an old friend who...." Mark broke off and looked as a door opened. It wasn't Sherrie.

"Forget it Mark." Kyle's voice was sharp.

"What's that Kyle?"

"I said forget it Mark. She's not coming."

Mark, a mix of puzzlement and fear on his face, looked at Kyle. He didn't say anything. Kyle studied Mark for a moment, then looked down at the flowers in his hand. Mark quickly placed them on the chair to his right, out of view.

"Sherrie Gammon will not be meeting you here tonight, Mark. Do you know why?"

Mark felt like he was going to throw up. "No, why Kyle?"

"Because she's not here. It's that simple. You've not been corresponding with her all this time."

"Wha... wha... what are you talking about Kyle?"

115

"Did it ever seem strange to you that Sherrie emailed you at work? How would she have gotten your email address?"

"Uh, uh, uh... I don't know Kyle! What are you saying?" Mark's mind was on the verge of shutting down. He felt claustrophobic. Like he wanted to get up and run out of the hotel and never stop running.

Kyle's voice became quiet, serious. "Listen, Mark. I got you your job at the company because I wanted to make sure my baby sister was well taken care of. As the IT Manager, it is my duty to monitor internet and email traffic. To make sure the employees comply with company policy with regard to internet usage. At the proxy server I can see where and when everyone is going. I saw you on a particular page on a particular website and put two and two together. So that's when I sent you the emails from 'Sherrie.'"

Mark became frantic. "That's spying Kyle! You have no right to invade my privacy like that!"

"Oh, but I do, Mark. It's my job. If you were at home on your own computer, I'd agree. But when you are at work, you are using the company's computer," Kyle paused, then with an edge of menace. "It's also my responsibility to watch out for Marissa."

Mark put his face into his hands. He was embarrassed, scared, and, strangely enough, relieved on some level. Then he told Kyle everything. His brother-in-law listened intently, nodding every now and then. When he was finished, Kyle leaned back in his chair and stared at the wall.

"I understand, Mark. Same thing happened to me a couple years back. Unfortunately, it nearly destroyed my marriage. And I found out that hooking up with an old girlfriend was simply a fantasy that I blew out of proportion. Turns out she wasn't the soul mate I had imagined her to be all that time."

Mark nodded in remembrance of that difficult period when Kyle and his wife separated for a while. He'd never known the details behind it; Kyle was a very private person.

"Look Kyle, I never wanted to hurt Marissa or the girls. I just felt like there was some unfinished business between me and Sherrie. Still do actually. But I wasn't going to leave Marissa or anything like that."

"Mark, the fantasy is often stronger than reality. You see Marissa every day. You see her bad side, her good side. Not so with the object of your fantasy. All you see there is mystery and excitement. It's a powerful lure, especially after being married for a long time. But it's a siren call, beckoning you to smash against hidden rocks."

Mark could see reason behind what Kyle was saying. He may have a yearn for the past, but it was Marissa who ultimately accepted Mark, who loved him despite his foibles. He looked at his watch. 5:37. He could still make it if traffic didn't hold him up too badly.

"Kyle, please please don't tell Marissa any of this. I feel terrible about it, and I'd hate for it to come out and hurt her."

Kyle smiled, held out his hand. "Count on it, bro-in-law."

Mark shook his hand and stood. "I have a recital to attend. Care to come along?"

"No, thank you. Think I'll grab a bite to eat and head home. See you Friday, Mark."

"Friday?"

"Yeah, company's sending me to tech training tomorrow."

Mark nodded, headed for the door. Before going through, he turned. "Thank you, Kyle."

Kyle gave a thumbs up. Then Mark left.

He drove like a man possessed. From the time he left the hotel to the time he pulled up into the school parking lot, Mark thought about the evening. A part of him was disappointed, both in not seeing Sherrie and also in himself. After all the years and questions he had about their relationship so long ago, he realized that some answers would never be known. Could never be known. In the scheme of his life, it didn't really matter, for he chose Marissa, and she was his soul mate.

Mark ran into the school's auditorium lobby just as people were filing in. He saw Marissa and Jessie standing at the entrance to the auditorium and called their names.

Marissa turned toward him a look of surprise on her face which quickly turned to delight. She ran over to Mark and threw her arms around his neck.

"Oh sweetheart, I'm so glad you're here. What happened to your meeting?"

Mark held her tightly. "Oh, I managed to beg my way out of it." He kissed her.

"Those are lovely flowers. Did you bring them for Erica?"

Mark pulled two roses from the bunch and handed one to Marissa and one to Jessie. Jessie squealed and hugged her dad.

"I brought them for all my girls. Now let's go watch the recital."

They went into the auditorium.

The next day at work, lunch hour came, and Mark logged on to oldfriendsreunited.com. He clicked on his old friends link, found Sherrie's name and clicked on it. When her page came up, her face was no longer there. There was, instead, a message which read, "This account has been cancelled."

Mark looked at the page until he saw his message tab on the website was blinking indicating a new message. He clicked on it. The message read:

Mark,

I noticed you have been to my site many times. I don't know if you realize it or not, but oldfriendsreunited.com automatically enters your name into my guestbook every time you open my page. Well I don't think it would be either good or appropriate to be in contact with each other at this time. I hope you understand. I wish you all the best.

Sincerely,
Sherrie Fischer

Mark read the note several times. Then he deleted it, turned his chair around and stared out the window until lunch hour ended.

THE BOX
(2008)

There's an elephant in the room.

Maybe elephant isn't the right word. Though it feels at times like an elephant, it's more like a box. A big box. Perhaps "white elephant" would be more fitting? But that doesn't seem right either. It doesn't seem right because though it has some value, its upkeep isn't a liability.

Or maybe it is.

Just knowing it's there is a liability. It forces me to think about it, something I'd rather not do at this time. But I can't ignore it.

It's a big box, and it demands my attention. I'll look away for a while.

If it isn't hanging on the periphery of my vision, it's slipping through the shadows of my knowledge. I can tell myself it's not there, but I know better. Looking away offers little in respite from the box.

"WHAT IS YOUR NAME?"

That voice again.

"My name is no different from the last time you asked," I reply, squinting into the darkness beyond the box. I think that's where the voice originated. Not sure.

"WHAT DO YOU DO?"

The voice asked that question before as well. I don't know what it wants for an answer. I work in advertising. I tried to tell it that, but it just asked the same question again.

"Why don't you come out of the darkness, so we can talk face to face?" I ask with some exasperation.

"WHY DO YOU DO?"

"Why do I do what!!?"
Then there is silence.
And the box.
I don't know where I am. I have a pretty good idea of how I got here, but I have no clue as to where "here" is. It was a strange, unexpected journey. There were airports, hours in a cramped tube at 35,000 feet. Back and forth. In between flights, there was a box. It was much like the box that commands this room.

"WHAT DO YOU DO?"

It asks again.
I think about it for a while. What do I do? I know what I used to do, and none of that seems useful any more.
"I...I...I used to be an artist," I reply hesitatingly.
There is nothing, no response. Just silence.
"Uhhh," I continue, "I used to write, so I guess I'm a writer."
My answers are weak, I know. I hadn't written or produced art in a long time. A long time. That box – I couldn't possibly concentrate on anything else while it dominates everything around it. Like I said earlier, it's the elephant in the room that no one wants to discuss.

No one, it seems, except me.

So I discuss it with myself. I consider it in the deepest, darkest moments, occasionally referring to photos or video if available. I talk about it from different angles – past, present, future, and I usually end up with a furtive sense of wistfulness for doing so.

"WHY DO YOU NOT DO?"

This question makes a light switch click on in my head. How often I had asked myself the same question, how often I found myself resignedly saying,

"I'm drained. I can't do any more. No, that's not quite right. It's more like I'm numb. It all seems so pointless to carry on the way I did before. Does that make sense? DOES THAT MAKE SENSE?"

I pause for a moment, awaiting a response that never comes. I should know better than to ask.

"Look, whoever you are… the box," I speak pointing to it. "That box needs to go – NO, it needs to stay. But I can't do anything as long as it's in here with me. It demands my attention. It makes me think about it. I was ill. I think the box did that. I'm better now, but nothing's different. The box still forces me to considerate it, to wonder about its sudden appearance. Who could've expected it? Boxes aren't uncommon – but look at that one! Just look at it! It's big. Big enough to crawl inside if I so wanted. I could stretch out in it; lie there comfortably looking like I had no more care than to sleep."

I was breathing heavily, as if I'd just run a marathon. My speech ran close, perilously close to something I'd never stated before. Perhaps given swift thought to, but never stated.

"WHAT IS YOUR NAME?"

"Uh, er, Donald J. Mulvey." I reply, finally, to this question. It's not as if it's a secret anyway.

"DONALD J. MULVEY, WHERE IS YOUR FATHER?"

I am taken aback by this question. I look around the room. I cast a glance at the box. A chill crawls up the back of my neck.
"I..I… don't…. know," I say slowly.
The questioner persists.

"DONALD J. MULVEY, WHERE IS YOUR FATHER?"

I can't answer the question. I won't answer the question. My father's whereabouts have everything – nothing – to do with this peculiar place in which I find myself. Yet, for some reason, I know why the voice is asking me this. It's not so much asking for a particular piece of knowledge as it is forcing me to… to….

look.

Wordlessly, I stagger to the box. It grows to immense, father-like proportions the closer I get to it. A strange, green glow seems to emanate from it, but I hear no hum of a Tesla generator or perpetual motion machine – all is silent, with the exception of my labored breathing.

I stand over the box. It's much smaller than I thought before. It's really only about the size of a large microwave oven. Maybe that's why it glows?

Kneeling next to the box, I breathe in deeply trying to slow my heart to normal. I look around me wildly to see if anyone or anything stands near. Nothing.

No one. I am alone.

"WHERE are you?" I finally get out.

Silence.

"Dad? Are you here?" I whisper.

Silence.

I look at the box. It is a cream-colored box, highly lacquered with shiny brass trim on its corners. The top of the box isn't flat. Rather it bulges upwards a bit as if to make more space for storage. There are brass handles on both sides. They look very practical for lifting and carrying the box.

The box looks like it has density, weight. It looks as if it would take at least four or six people to lift it.

Tentatively, I reach out and touch it. It is smooth, cool. There is a fine thrumming feeling in it that transfers up through my fingers, along my arm and vibrates the back of my shoulder. I snatch my hand back as if I had just accidentally touched a hidden puff adder.

"WHAT IS IT?" I shriek at the top of my lungs.

I don't want to be in that room with the box. I don't want to open it and look inside. For some reason, I feel like I would be shattered from inside out if I did. Yet, I need to know. I am compelled by the voice's complicit silence to carry through to the end.

I extend my hand to the lid of the box. Closing my eyes, I grasp a handle, lift it up.

The thrumming I felt earlier going up my arm now seems to be centered in my chest. I half expect to hear a haunted house creaking sound, but the lid rises easily, soundlessly.

Clenching my teeth, I slowly open my eyes. I can feel my knuckles turn white as my grip on the handle hardens. I breathe in quickly at what I see…. then let out a slow breath.

Sitting on a bed of sand inside the box is a turtle shell. I reach in, grab its textured smoothness and lift it out of the box. It is very light. When I hold it up to the light, I can see that it is empty. Who or whatever inhabited that shell was long gone, leaving behind the burden that was its home and protection as it crawled the sands of our world.

"WHAT IS IN THE BOX, DONALD J. MULVEY?"

The voice came suddenly, causing me to jump a little.

I answer, "It's empty. That's what it is… empty. It once was, now it's not. It's my heart. It's my soul. It was life, now it's nonlife. It's not even death; I could handle that. It's just nonlife. It's a hole."

I sigh; set the shell on the floor beside me. I draw my legs up to my chest and wrap my arms around them.

Then I rock.

And rock.

And rock.

****

"Well, what do you think?" Brad asked Gary, the small, silent man standing next to him.

"We don't know, yet, exactly what happened, and we definitely aren't getting any answers out of Mr. Mulvey for the time being," responded Gary. "His father was named Donald J. Mulvey. Did you know that?"

Brad turned to look through the one-way window at Donald sitting on the floor, rocking back and forth to some toneless tune in his head.

"No, I didn't know that. That would make our guest here a junior, I suppose. Wonder why he didn't include that when he answered the name question."

Gary continued, "We found Mr. Mulvey, Sr. in Jr's apartment. He was dead. Autopsy is being conducted right now. Mr. Mulvey, Jr. was sitting at an easel in the same room as his father's body. He was working on a painting."

Brad watched Donald pick up the overturned plastic bowl and place it back in the cardboard box in front of him. He murmured, "What was the painting of?"

"Well, it was the oddest thing. As far as we can tell, he was painting a picture of his dead father's body, a sort of a portrait I suppose."

"Oh?"

"Yeah, it was a pretty good rendition too, except he made his dad's skin look like rough leather or scaly. Not only that, but he gave him a huge hump on his back. It looks like he was trying to paint his dad into a turtle. But the picture wasn't finished yet, so we're not sure. We'll try asking him later today."

"Good luck. All he seems to want to do is play with that box and plastic bowl."

****

They think I don't know they're watching me. They think I'm crazy or something, I suppose. Doesn't really matter what they think, though. We are all just turtles anyway. They are. I am. My father was. And some day, we'll all be shells, smooth and clean for the taking.

126

Just shells. Unable to reach out and touch, unable to feel or love, we will time pass the golden stamp of our aura in the space we inhabit. As our personal space grows impersonal, others will remark at how good we look, how much we'll be missed. If we are lucky. But we won't know.

Won't know. Because we are just shells. Inanimate. Cold, unyielding.

No one likes to think about it.

But I do.

And I need to look again.

And again.

I can't seem to stop.

A FOREST IN FOREVER
(2008)

"Funny Face, dontcha know? Remember that?" Dave asked. "Goofy Grape, Choo Choo Cherry, Rootin' Tootin' Raspberry?"

"Nah," I replied. "We was strickly ZaRex."

"ZaRex, hmmmphh! You was from the rich side of town, then. We couldn't afford that syrupy stuff," Dave replied.

"Pshaw! You want any more ice tea?" I said, standing up from the rocking chair I'd been sitting in since lunch.

"Yeah, I'll take one more, if you don't mind," Dave answered.

I walked into the store, Bragdon's Variety of East Turnbull, Maine. It was an old store, been in East Turnbull since the 1950s. My son, Steve, bought it three years ago when he moved back here from Chicago with his family in tow. Steve's wife, Janice, was a pretty little thing, but without a whit of common sense, I thought. His children, Donnie, Vanessa and Timothy took a while getting used to living in rural Maine where there weren't a whole lot of conveniences nearby like in the city. But kids are adaptable, even if they are teenagers, and they managed to finally settle in. Probably got some help from the video game console I bought them for Christmas last year – seems like that's what they do most of the time.

Dave and I spent a lot of afternoons sitting on the porch of the store jawing back and forth. He had lost his wife to cancer five years back, and mine was in a fatal car accident which is why Steve came home to Maine. He gave up a good job in an accounting firm to return to his roots. Said he wanted to be near in case I needed him, but I think he was really getting tired of the city more than anything else.

I fetched two ice teas from the cooler and stopped at the cash register to pay for them. Bonnie, the cashier, smiled and shook her head.

"Don't worry about it Mr. Hughes. It's on the house."

"Why thanky, Bonnie," I smiled back at her. "S'bout time for you to be heading back to school, ain't it?"

"I'm leaving in a week. Tomorrow's my last day here until next summer." Bonnie replied.

"Orono is it?" She nodded. "What's Stevie gonna do once you're gone? You're his right hand man, so to speak."

"My mom is going to come in and work. She said she could use the extra money. Not much to do now that tourist season is winding down anyway."

"Ayuh, it does get a bit quieter here after August. Thanks again, dear."

I went out onto the front porch and handed Dave his ice tea. The rocking chair creaked resignedly as I settled back down into it. We were silent for a while as we sipped our cold drinks. The store sat on Route 4 where it skirted Turnbull Pond, so we had a nice view of the water from here. The road was usually quite busy during deep summer but became almost deserted as the days grew shorter and cooler right before September.

"I hear Joe's finally moved south like he always said he was gonna do," Dave broke the silence. Joe was my next door neighbor, if you can call being six hundred feet away as next door.

"Yup. He packed up his stuff, threw Ginny in the car and left for North Carolina a coupla weeks ago. Said he wasn't sticking around for one more winter. His house is for sale. Ted Guerrette Real Estate outta Auburn's trying to sell it for him."

"Can't say as I blame him. Winter ain't for us old folks no more. It's getting tougher to get through it. I've been thinking 'bout moving myself."

I looked at Dave. He was gazing out toward the pond, a far away look on his face.

"Now Dave. You ain't been farther south than Kittery. You have Maine granite in your bones. If you died down south, where would you be buried? Thought you had a plot next to Lisa's?"

He looked at me, but his eyes still seemed to be focusing on something in the distance. His face was sort of sad. "That's the only reason I stuck around here for the last five years, Harm. If I moved away, I wouldn't be able to visit Lisa like I can now. But it's awful hard – you should know. When Lisa died, my house stopped being a home. It's just a place for me to live and nothin' else." Dave sat back in his chair, wiped the back of his hand across his eyes.

I knew what he was saying. I always thought I'd rather have lost Maggie to a long illness than a car accident. At least I would have had time to prepare. But in the end, it's all the same. We had to deal with the empty spot in our lives, try to figure out a way to fill it again until we came to realize that it would never be filled. At least not in the way it had been filled before. Death wasn't just about loss; it was about change as well. I found that time wasn't the wound healer everyone said it was. More than anything, it just took some of the edge off like an aspirin might ease a headache for a while.

We didn't speak much more after that. Dave finished his tea, tossed the bottle into the returns box by the door and said his goodbyes. I watched him slowly climb into his old Chevy, then waved to him as he turned north on to Rt. 4. As his car disappeared around a bend in the road, another car pulled into the small parking lot in front of the store. The driver got out, gave a half wave. I waved back.

"Hi Dad!" Steve said as he bounded up the steps to the porch and sat down in the chair where Dave had been.

"How's things going Stevie?"

"Oh good. Has it been busy this afternoon?"

"There's been a few customers, mostly Massachusetts folks stopping by for their Megabucks tickets before heading home for the year." Megabucks lottery tickets were only sold in Maine, New Hampshire and Vermont. By far, tourists from Massachusetts bought up the most tickets while they were here. I have my own thoughts about government-sponsored gambling, but I won't say good or bad of it to most. The folks who come into the store to buy tickets usually pick up something else as well, so it's benefited my son.

"I'll miss the tourists," Steve said somberly.

"It's a tough way to make a living," I agreed. "But, hey, when NuBalance builds that new plant just down the road a ways, you'll have all kinds of business."

"Dad, that's been talked about since we moved here. Nothing's happened, though, and I can't make any money off speculative discussions," he paused for a minute or so. "I'm thinking about selling the store and moving to Portland." He looked at me expectantly.

I nodded, considering his statement. "Well Stevie. Can't say I'm surprised. Is it just because of business?"

Steve shook his head. "No, not just. I'd also like to get the kids into neighborhoods where there are a lot of other kids their age they can do things with. And Janice has never really adjusted well to living out here in the sticks."

"Ayuh, you either like it or you don't," I replied. "You grew up here, though - seemed to do okay with it."

"I guess it's just what you get used to," Steve smiled. "Yeah, I loved it here. Thought there was no better place on earth to live. But I discovered there's a whole lot more out there than I could have imagined when I went to college in Massachusetts."

I thought about that for a bit. Guess if I was honest, I'd have to say I felt the same way when I was younger. But things change as you grow older and what seemed so important before wouldn't merit a space on the top shelf of your closet when you've got a lot less life ahead of you than behind. I tried a different tack.

"You could move to Lewiston or Auburn and still not be too far away," I proposed. Suddenly, it seemed to me like everyone wanted to leave East Turnbull except me.

"Janice doesn't really like LA much. Not enough cultural stuff, not like *Portland*," Steve sighed and rolled his eyes at the same time.

"Well, you do what you have to do, Stevie," I turned to stare out over the pond and chugged down the last of my ice tea.

"Speaking of that," he said looking at his watch. "I have to get inside and relieve Bonnie for the night. Are you going to stick around?"

"Nah. Think I'll just amble on home in a sec."

"Where's your car? I didn't see it coming in."

"Don't have it. I came here through the woods out back."

"Dad! You know you shouldn't be walking the woods trail between here and your house. It's about a mile and there's no one around to hear you if you fall and need help."

132

I smiled at his concern. It was really misplaced and a bit specious as well. At 75, I was still in pretty good shape; took a long walk every day and ate well. Years of sawmill work had hardened me to the point where I didn't want to get soft, so I stayed active. I've seen too many folks my age allow themselves to dwindle down to failure.

"The woods trail is a good one. Helped build it myself with Cy Woodruff who owned this store back in the 60s. Tain't nothing more dangerous in them woods than a few skunks and some deer. Maybe an odd fisher cat, too."

"Okay Dad," Steve held up his hands. "Can you at least carry a cell phone when you do it?"

I pulled my light jacket back, so he could see the phone clipped to my belt.

"I may be daring, but I'm not stupid, Stevie."

"Good, good, call me if you need anything, OK?"

"Will do, son."

He reached over and gave me a quick man's hug. I patted his back, said goodbye. Then I stepped down off that porch where I'd been sitting most of the afternoon and hiked out behind the store. There was a short field to go through before the woods. The grass was high, dotted mostly with Queen Ann's lace, sorrel, burdock and jimson weed. In amongst the jimson, I saw a few small teaberry plants, pulled off some leaves and stuck them in my mouth. I always liked having something to chew as I walked; it helped keep my mouth from getting thirsty.

Plunging into the woods was like walking into a cellar with the light off, it was that dense. The trail was wide and clear of brush. It didn't wander much, so I never worried about getting off it somehow. But I still had to stop for a few moments to let my eyes adjust to the much darker surroundings. Taking a deep breath, I could smell the deep, resinous fragrance of the pines. They were towering things; would have been perfect for ships' masts back in the early 1800s. Of course, they weren't as large back then as they are now, and some didn't even exist. But there were trees very much like this fueling Maine's shipbuilding economy.

My eyes were finally adjusted, so I started walking the trail. It wasn't long before I was lost in thought. The stillness of the forest does that to me, allows my mind to wander and focus in on its wanderings. It shields me from the world around it as it envelopes me, dulls some senses, sharpens others.

I was somewhat concerned with what I perceived to be a growing exodus from East Turnbull. I suppose the feeling was enhanced by the ending of summer with all the tourists heading home. At times it made me feel like the janitor who is left to clean up after a wedding reception. But Joe's leaving, and Dave and Steve talking about leaving was a different matter altogether. I'd known Joe for twenty-three years since he first moved into the old farmhouse next to my field. I'd been best friends with Dave longer than that.

It wasn't just them, however. They were the straws that were really putting a bend in the camel's back. Over the years, I've watched as long time residents left the area for one reason or another. The Lamberts left ten years ago when Phil accepted a job in Cleveland. Missy Herman took her two youngsters and moved to Lewiston when Stu, her tosspot of a husband, drowned himself in Turnbull Pond trying to snowmobile across rotten ice in early spring last year. Del Clinton sold the old family homestead with all its acreage to a developer who put up a bunch of cookie-cutter townhouses on the knoll that overlooks the far end of the pond. Del ran off with the money to Vegas or Atlantic

City, I suppose. No one's seen or heard from him again.

Growing up in East Turnbull, I could always count on stability. Now it seemed like change was the norm, and I was a bit sadder for it.

"Feeling sorry for yourself again, Harmon Hughes?"

That voice!

It always made me jump. You think I'd be used to it by now.

"Took you long enough to show up, Maggie," I said with a sideways look of bemusement.

"I… was… busy," she replied coquettishly.

"Well, I've missed you something fierce!" I stopped in my tracks and put my arms around her. She melted into my embrace. We held onto each other as if we were lifebuoys in a turbulent ocean.

"I've missed you, too," she whispered.

After a few minutes, we let go. Maggie took my hand. We started walking the trail to home.

"Why haven't you left, Harm?" she finally asked.

"Oh Maggie, Maggie. Dear, why would I leave you? And where would I go?"

"Away, honey. Away. There's no one and nothing for you in East Turnbull anymore. Your friends are mostly gone or dead. The only family that's here - Steve - is talking about leaving. After he goes, what's left for you?"

"Don't talk that way, Maggie! I used to, but as long as I can see you, I have my whole world."

"But I don't know how long that will be, sweetest."

"Why? Do you have a time limit?" I felt a seam of fear chill up through my soul.

Maggie pulled away from me a few feet. She twirled in the trail; her dress flowed out from her like a ballet dancer's.

She smiled sweetly at me.

"Nothing lasts forever, love of mine." Maggie laughed. It sounded like wind chimes in a warm summer evening breeze.

"Maybe not, but forever lasts a lot longer when you're around," I replied. I began chasing her among the trees where she laughingly flitted like a wraith. We were heading into the deep forest, away from the trail. I knew where she was going; we'd been there numerous times before.

There was an old hunting cabin back beyond the ridge that ran generally northwest along East Turnbull's town line. It had belonged to Cy Woodruff. We built the trail to connect it to our houses and the store. The portion of the trail that led out to the cabin had long since grown over as nature reclaimed its own. Cy had passed on years ago, so the cabin was abandoned. I don't even know if the current owner realizes it's there, and I've never let on anything about it.

As we neared the cabin in our game of chase, I stopped short.

"What's that I hear?" I asked in disbelief.

Maggie slinked over to me and leaned against my side.

"I made some arrangements, darling," she said huskily.

As we stepped into the clearing, I gazed into the sky. It was dark, like night, but my watch said it was only about 5:00 PM. It shouldn't be getting dark until about 7:30, yet there were stars in the sky. A full moon shone down on the cabin, which I could see in the distance. Its windows, long since broken out by vandals, glowed with a warm gold light. There was a lovely stream of music flowing lazily through the air. I think it was *Moonlight Serenade* playing.

"Wow, honey," was all I could think to say.

"Do you like?" she smiled.

"Oh, ayuh. This is wonderful!"

Arm in arm we walked slowly toward the cabin. The music wrapped all around us, though I could see no source for it. The air was sweet with pine and fresh, clean night air - the type of air that is harbinger for the coming autumn. Through the cabin windows, I could see a warm, cozy room lit by many candles. Maggie slipped her arm around my waist. I pulled her closer. Our steps matched one another's.

Just as we reached the door, my cell phone rang.

"Hold on a minute, Maggie," I said. Speaking into the phone, "Yeah?"

"Dad!"

"Stevie?"

"Yeah, Dad. Just thought I'd call to see if you made it home okay."

"Stevie, I'm just fine, thank you."

"Is that music I hear playing?"

"Yeah, Stevie... listen, I'm with your mom right now. I'll call you back later."

There was a brief silence. "Dad?"

"Yeah, what?"

"Dad, Mom died three years ago."

I sighed.

"Don't you think I know that Stevie?"

"So, what do you mean that you are with Mom?"

"I'll try to explain it to you later, Stevie, OK? Goodbye." I was getting a little impatient with this conversation.

"But, Da..." I turned off the phone, folded it shut and returned it to my belt.

Smiling at Maggie, I motioned to the door and said, "Shall we?"

"Love to," she smiled back.

I opened the door. Then I picked her up and carried her into the cabin. She giggled like a teenager as I kicked the door closed behind us.

****

Steve reached for his beeping cell phone which sat on the counter beside the cash register. The beep indicated a text message had been received. Steve opened the phone, pushed a button and read the text on the small screen.

"I'm leaving. Love you. Dad."

Steve frowned at the message. He dialed his father's cell phone number. There was no answer, so he left a voicemail message. Steve then tried his father's home phone. No answer there either. It wasn't like his dad to be impulsive like this. He usually gave good, clear notice of his intentions. The text message, coupled with that bizarre statement an hour or so before, had Steve worried. He decided to close the store early – most of the regulars had already stopped by to get their beer and cigarettes for the night – and go to his father's house.

Though the house was a mile away through the woods, it was a three mile drive by paved road. Steve could have cut off some of the distance by taking old dirt roads, but his car just wouldn't have made it. Even so, it didn't take long to make the circuitous route.

The house was tucked back into the treeline at the rear of the property. No lights were on; the car was parked in the gravel driveway. If he left, shouldn't the car be gone as well?

Steve pulled into the driveway a bit too fast. When he

hit the brakes, the tires broke free of the gravel surface, and his car slid into his dad's with a thump. One of Steve's headlights went out.

Oh no! I'll have to worry about that later, Steve thought. He jumped out of his car, ran up to the front door and didn't bother knocking. Instead he used a key to let himself in. There was no sound in the house.

"Dad!" Nothing.

"Dad! Are you here!?" Steve started walking through the house, turning on lights as he went. Everything looked normal. There was no indication of a departure, hurried or leisurely. Clothes still hung in the bedroom closet or were folded neatly in drawers. Toiletries were still on the bathroom shelves. When Steve opened the medicine cabinet, he saw the prescription medicines his dad had to take for blood pressure and cholesterol.

"Everything is still here," Steve pondered. "Nothing missing that I can see, so where is he?"

Then it hit him.

The woods!

He sprang to the door, threw it open.

"Whoa, Stevie-boy! It's dark out there. You need a flashlight to do what you want to do."

Steve had no idea where his dad kept a flashlight, so he rummaged through all the drawers and closets until he finally found one. It was a large Maglite that put out a strong beam. Switching it on, Steve stepped outside. He looked at its bright beam illuminating everything at which he pointed it. Using it, he made his way around the house to the opening of the wood trail.

"Dad!" Steve yelled.

The only response was the crickets' chirp.

Taking a deep breath, Steve plunged into the woods.

At first he was impressed at how smooth the trail was, how easy it was to walk it. Then he was cursing as he spat out a mouth full of pine needles and dirt that he'd almost swallowed when he tripped over a tree root and fell forward to the ground. It wouldn't do to stumble along the trail while flashing the light into the woods. So he decided to light the path for twenty steps, stop, look around and yell. This way Steve made it deep into the forest, but it took quite a while to get anywhere.

If I was smart, I'd just wait until morning to do a search, he thought. *No. What if Dad was lying hurt somewhere along the trail? Maybe his text message was some kind of warning - maybe he's fatally injured!*

This last thought made Steve stop in his tracks. He switched off the light for a minute and listened. The absolute darkness of the woods closed in around him suffocatingly. With the exception of a breeze in the tree tops and an occasional hoot of an owl somewhere in the distance, he couldn't hear anything.

Maybe, there are bears or wolves!

Steve immediately turned the light on and spun around in a circle. Rough tree trunks sprang into sharp relief as the beam passed them; it did little to penetrate beyond the immediate area, though.

He started walking the trail again, this time keeping his light on the ground ahead of him. Calling out periodically and listening the rest of the time, Steve was able to make it to the field behind the store in good time. He had not seen, nor heard anything while in the woods that would lead him to believe his father was lying under a tree somewhere dying

Perhaps he's already dead?

That was a possibility. But there was no real reason for it. Harmon Hughes was in great shape for a man 40 years old, let alone 75. The only thing Steve nagged his dad about was his eyesight. He had shown signs of not being able to see as well as he used to. Otherwise, he had no severe medical issues, no chronic diseases. There was virtually no reason for the man's heart to simply stop beating.

Wild animals?

While his dad always insisted there was nothing more dangerous than deer in those woods, Steve had heard stories from locals coming into the store about coyotes, foxes and bear roaming within the town's boundaries. Neighbors' cats had disappeared. Something had tried to dig under the chicken coop fence at Hal Wilson's place just the other night. Hal lived on the other side of town, but wild animals roam, don't they?

What about murder?

East Turnbull was a quiet town - not much criminal activity took place here. Still, it wasn't totally out of the question. The only thing that made Steve have doubts was the nature of Dad's message: "I'm leaving. Love you. Dad."

That just didn't sound like someone in the throes of being the victim of a violent act. Steve had a lot of questions. He wished his dad had taken the time to prepare him for this. He was unsure of what to do now, so he went into the store and called the Androscoggin County Sheriff's office to file a missing person's alert. A deputy was dispatched to the store to question Steve.

When the deputy arrived, Steve took him to the entrance of the trail, told him everything he knew. There wasn't really much to tell. As it was getting late, the deputy offered to give Steve a ride back to his car. The offer was gladly accepted.

"There will be a search party organized in the morning," the deputy said. "We will base it out of your store and scour the woods between it and your dad's house. If we have to, we can bring in dogs to track. See if you can find an unwashed article of clothing that belonged to your dad."

Steve agreed and thanked the deputy. He stepped out of the car - they were already in his dad's driveway - and watched as the car drove away. Then he walked to the trail entrance behind the house. It was dark outside, but the woods were darker. There was a deepness to it that seemed secretive, not really evil, but mischievous. Steve was sure the answer was in there somewhere.

"This is like something out of a scary, campfire story," he murmured. A cold breeze blew out of the woods as if in response. Steve shuddered, went back to his car and drove home.

Bragdon's Variety was a beehive of activity the following day. Three search parties were formed to search along the trail and both sides of it. If Harmon had stumbled off the trail into the woods, they should find him quickly. An injured man wouldn't be able to travel far. Steve wanted to join the search, but he had to remain at the store until Bonnie came in at 1:00.

After two full sweeps of the mile-long trail with widening search parameters had turned up nothing, the search parties returned to the store for coffee and to discuss strategy. Sheriff Guy Levesque handed a deputy a topographical map and gave him instructions as to where to deploy the parties. Then he went into the store.

"We are going to send a party to your dad's house to do a thorough search inside and in the woods immediately around it. Another party will search the woods south of the trail all the way to Weston Road. The third party will wait for Gary Smalley to bring his tracking dog and backtrack the trail again," he told Steve.

Steve nodded. He handed the sheriff a large cup of fresh coffee.

"Thank you much, Mr. Hughes. If your dad is anywhere within three miles of this store, we'll find him."

"Thank you Sheriff. I really appreciate everything you are doing. It probably isn't anything but some sort of misunderstanding. Maybe my dad will just show up this afternoon like he usually does every day and wonder what all the fuss is about."

Sheriff Levesque smiled. "Well, if that happens, we'll all be the better for it." He went out the door. Just as the door closed, it opened again. The deputy Steve had spoken with the night before popped in. Steve could hear a dog barking outside.

"Mr. Hughes. Did you bring the article of clothing I mentioned last night?"

Steve reached down behind the counter and brought up a paper bag.

"This is it. I didn't touch anything with my hands, wore gloves to put them in this paper bag. There are a couple items that I took out of his dirty clothes hamper."

"Great, great. We'll just let Maggie get a good sniff of these, and we'll be off."

"Maggie??" Steve asked incredulously. His face flushed and a weird sensation crawled down his neck.

"Yeah, she's Gary Smalley's beagle we use for this sort of thing. You know... tracking. Are you okay?"

"Yeah, I'm okay. Maggie is... is…well, it *was* the name of my mother also."

The deputy nodded. "Well, maybe that's a good sign then. We'll let you know as soon as we find something." He went outside.

Steve followed him out onto the porch. He watched as the deputy led the search party around to the back of the store. Then he sat down in his dad's rocker. A few seconds later, he heard the baying of the beagle fade away and assumed that the party had gone into the woods. A short-lived silence fell on the store, broken when a car pulled into the parking lot.

Dave emerged from the car. He joined Steve on the porch, sitting in his usual spot.

"What's going on Steve? Where's Harm?" He asked.

"Haven't you heard? Dad's disappeared."

Dave sat quietly for a minute, a blank look on his face.

He said slowly, "So he's finally gone and done it."

Steve sat up straight, looked at Dave intently.

"Gone and done what Dave?"

Dave had a troubled look on his face. "I don't know 'zactly what Steve, but your dad's talked about leaving East Turnbull."

"Is that it Dave?? A lot of people TALK about leaving. You've talked about leaving. I've talked about leaving. I don't think I've heard one person talk about *staying!*" Steve's voice grew shrill.

Dave was conciliatory, "Now, now Steve. Calm down. Tain't nothing, I'm thinking. It's just that since your dad started mentioning that he was seeing your mom, well I just thought that…"

Immediately Steve was on his feet and leaning over Dave. "WHAT DO YOU MEAN – SEEING MY MOM??!"

Dave stared at Steve. He cocked his head to one side. Reaching up with both hands, he gently pushed Steve back.

"Set down Steve. We need to talk."

144

Steve took a deep breath and sat down. He rubbed his face with his hands and waited for Dave to talk. Dave pulled out his pipe, took some time to put tobacco in it and tamp it down. He lit it, took a couple puffs, then began.

"Around the beginning of the summer, Harmon started walking the woods trail as he liked to do in nice weather. Well, it wasn't long before he started making comments about seeing Maggie again. I thought maybe it was just wishful thinking or maybe I heard him wrong. But one day, he said to me,

'Dave, I saw her again. I saw Maggie.'

And I said back to him, 'Oh really Harm? Now just where would this have been?'

And he says, 'In the woods, along the trail.'

I asked him, 'You taking to seeing ghosts Harm?'

'No Dave. It ain't a ghost. It's her, I touched her.'

He seemed insistent that he was seeing Maggie. I was afraid that maybe Alzheimer's or dementia was starting to settle in. But he never acted strange otherwise, and I figured that if he was failing, it woulda been obvious in most ways he acted."

Dave paused to think about what he'd said. He puffed on his pipe.

Then he continued.

"Harm said he could only see her in the woods out back, that she never came home with him. And she wouldn't come to the store either. I thought he musta been spinning me a yarn the whole time, like he used to do when he was younger and trickier. But he seemed so earnest, so happy again. And I felt even more lonely in losing Lisa. So I just sat here and said, 'yeah?' from time to time while he was talking."

Steve was stunned. He didn't know what to think or say. His father must have been hallucinating; it was obvious. Maybe the medication he took? None of the drugs were psychotropic or narcotic, though. His doctor would surely know about the possibility of drug interactions as well.

"Dave, my dad mentioned he was with my mom last night. Now he's missing. I thought he... I don't know what I thought. His saying so just sort of freaked me out. I can only hope that the search teams find him in the woods somewhere, and he is still alive."

Dave leaned forward, his arms on his knees. He stared at the floor for a few minutes. It appeared that he was thinking hard.

He finally said, "Steve. I think I might just know where your father is."

Steve perked up. "Where, Dave?"

"Off in the woods, just over the ridge that runs that way," Dave motioned nonchalantly with his left hand. "There's a cabin; the Woodruff cabin. It's an old hunting cabin that Cy used to use every year. I been out there a few times myself when the guys around here took a couple weeks off in November to set up a deer camp."

"Can you still find the cabin, Dave?"

"I believe I could, if I hadta. It's been a long time though. Haven't been out there since Cy died and my arthritis came on."

"Well, if the search parties return without Dad, would you at least tell them about the cabin?"

"Oh yeah. I shouldn't, but I will."

"Why shouldn't you?"

"I promised your dad a couple weeks ago I wouldn't. I think he's been going there with your mom... or her ghost, or whatever."

Steve shivered as he tried to imagine it. His dad had always been level-headed, no-nonsense and chock full of common sense. It seemed unlikely that grief would make him create an imaginary image of his wife in order to cope. On the other hand, powerful emotions can cause odd effects in a person. Psychosomatic illnesses, multiple personalities - the mind often has a strange way of reinterpreting reality into something potentially damaging if only to subvert pain for a while.

"Well, if you can just let the Sheriff know, I'm sure Dad would understand."

Neither man spoke again until one of the search parties returned. The beagle leading the party announced their presence as they appeared around the corner of the store. As the group mingled in the parking lot, the deputy came over to the porch and spoke with Steve.

"Darndest thing happened out there," he began. "Maggie found the scent pretty quickly in that field behind the store, got real excited around some jimson weed. As bad as that stuff smells, I'm surprised she kept the scent. Then she beelined for the woods and took us down the trail a few hundred feet. At that point, she acted like she was confused and kept wanting to come back. I gave her another whiff of the clothing and she started sniffing around again. Then she would whine, turn around in a circle and lie down in the trail. We tried searching out into the woods in that area, but didn't see anything."

Dave spoke up, "Did you see a small triangular piece of plywood tacked to one of the trees along the trail there? It would be quite gray and weathered."

The deputy thought for a moment. "Aye, we did at that. Andy made mention of it, pointed it out. But we didn't think anything of it. How did you know?"

"It was the marker for the entrance to another trail that's probably grown over by now." Dave told the deputy everything he had told Steve with regard to the cabin. He didn't mention anything about Harm and Maggie. When he had finished, the deputy called one of the men over.

"Andy, you have that map? Dave, can you show us on a map the whereabouts of that cabin?"

Dave said he could. After orienting himself to the map, he circled his finger over the general area of where the cabin was located. The party had gathered around, watching his movements.

One of the men interjected, "Is that the old Woodruff cabin? I think I know where it is. It ain't far from the Hundred Acre Swamp. A guy could get lost in there."

A new sense of excitement rippled through everyone. The deputy quickly started giving orders.

"Tom, you're going to lead us to the cabin. We will search there first. If we find nothing, then we will start searching the swamp. We'll need to stay together out there and be able to signal if someone gets lost. Andy, I want you to stay behind here and marshal up the other search parties when they return. Send them to the cabin. We'll get everyone together there and reestablish our search parameters. Mr. Hughes, Dave... would either of you like to go with us?"

Steve and Dave looked at each other for a moment. A sense of understanding passed between them that could not be seen or known by anyone else. It was the feeling that the searchers were going to intrude on something very private.

"I think we'll remain here," Steve said.

"Yeah," agreed Dave.

"OK, everyone knows what we are going to do. Let's head out!"

The search party went back to the woods with much

animation and chatter.

Steve and Dave didn't watch them, preferring instead to gaze out over the pond.

"Ice tea, Dave?"

"Yes, thank you Stevie."

Steve smiled at that and went inside to get ice teas.

By the time the deputy returned from the search, Dave had left. Bonnie was behind the cash register, and Steve was sitting in the chair on the porch.

"We found him, Mr. Hughes," the deputy said solemnly.

Steve could tell the news wasn't good.

"Please, call me Steve."

"Oh… you can call me Hank," the deputy, surprised, held out his hand. Steve shook it. "Anyway, we found his body in the cabin. His wallet still had some money in it along with his driver's license. Tom, one of the guys in the group, has some EMT training, so he checked your dad over. There's no evidence of trauma or injury. It looks like he may have just had a heart attack. I have to call in a couple ATV's with a stretcher wagon to get him out of there. It's a ways back in, and the terrain is not real easy to walk."

"Is that it, Hank? Was there anything else?"

"Well, his cell phone was still in his hand. I brought it with me. Tom also found some chewed substance in his mouth. It was green, looked like it might have been plant material. Did your dad ever pick plants to chew on?"

Steve thought for a moment.

"Yeah, he was always finding teaberry or wintergreen plants. He liked to chew them, especially while on hunting trips."

"That might explain Maggie's behavior around the

jimson weed out back. There was a smattering of teaberry there among the jimson," Hank stopped for a moment to consider what he just said. "You know, if your dad accidentally pulled off a piece of the jimson and chewed it, it could cause hallucinations."

"Huh?" Steve felt a rush go through him.

"Jimson weed is sometimes used by Native Americans in religious rituals to bring on visions, to see people that aren't really there and communicate with them. Too much of it can kill a person. And it doesn't take much to make too much, if you get my drift."

That must be it! That's why Dad saw Mom, or claimed he did.

"Hmmm, Hank. I was on my dad a lot to get his eyes checked out. I think his vision was deteriorating. But he'd never go to the doctor for it," Steve said, slowly.

"Well, an autopsy will be performed on him, and we'll request a toxicology report as well. But I'm pretty sure that's what we're dealing with here. Your father probably grabbed some jimson, chewed it and wandered the forest in a delirium until he ended up at that cabin and just died."

Steve was relieved to have a logical answer. Strangely, though, he also felt disappointment. Accidental overdose seemed so urban, so unromantic. So tragic.

"Hank, could I possibly have Dad's cell phone?"

Hank considered the request. "I really shouldn't. It could be considered evidence in a potential crime scene."

"Do you really think this is a crime scene?"

"No Steve, I don't. But there are procedures that we're supposed to follow. Was there any particular reason you wanted it?"

"I just wanted to see if there were any pictures stored on it. It had a camera built into it."

"Well, just give me your email address, and I'll send you the photos. How's that sound?"

"That would be great, Hank. Thanks a lot."

They shook hands again. Hank went to his patrol car and started sending radio messages to dispatch. Steve looked out over the pond. East Turnbull wouldn't be the same any more, not without his dad here. Thomas Wolfe was right - you can't go home again. Perhaps he was a fool to drag his family here from Chicago. It had been with the noblest of intentions to get them out of crazy city life and into something less hectic. But that was, in a way, like forcing a coffee drinker to switch to decaf.

Steve was unable to recapture the essence of life in East Turnbull the way he remembered it as a child. Now the final ties to it were severed, and he was actually thinking that Portland may not be such a bad idea after all.

Two weeks later, Steve was on his computer at home. He stared at the photos that he'd just received from Hank. The email message read:

Steve,

There were only three pictures on the cell phone. I have attached them to this email. They are a little difficult to make out, but I don't think there is anything about them that's conclusive with regards to the case. I also put a copy of the autopsy report to you in the mail. You should be receiving it in a few days. My sincerest condolences for the loss of your father.

Regards,

Hank Strother, Deputy
Androscoggin County Sheriff's Department

The three pictures that were difficult for Hank to make out were clear as glass to Steve. Though the pictures were low in resolution and rather grainy, he could see that they were of his mother many years ago. In fact, they were almost carbon copies of pictures that Harmon Hughes took of Maggie Hughes (née Ouellette) while they were honeymooning at Niagara Falls. Steve remembered the pictures well from the photo albums he used to pore over as a child. He could make out candles in the honeymoon suite in one picture. And the other two were apparently from some hiking trails somewhere in or near Niagara. That was back in the quaint days when women wore dresses for outdoor activities, impractical as it was.

He wondered why his dad would take cell phone pictures of old photographs.

"Dad's heart just stopped. That's what the autopsy report said. There was no indication of heart attack, artery blockage or scarring. He just died, that's all," Steve shrugged.

Dave and Steve were sitting on the front porch of the store. It was late Friday afternoon, mid-September. The days were still warm, but the evenings were cooling down. There was a nip in the air at night which echoed in the soul's hall of change. They were in the transitional season, that time when all of nature is in movement to prepare for the coming winter. Geese were starting to fly overhead, honking chaotically as they went. Leaves of hardwood trees were turning from summer green to brilliant yellows and reds, but only in select places. Full color wouldn't come for another couple weeks. School buses were running again after their summer hibernation.

"I miss Harm, Stevie. He was a good friend, the best," Dave stated. "Did the report have any other information?"

Steve hesitated before answering. Maybe some things weren't nice and neat after all. Maybe you couldn't explain everything away with logic and sense. Life always seemed to create more questions than it answered.

"The toxicology report came up negative. The leaves in his mouth were teaberry, not jimson." Steve finally said as he reached for his bottle of ice tea. It was starting to get dark out. A chilly breeze blew off the pond across the road from the store. Both men were lost in thought, saying nothing for a long time. Without speaking, they knew they were thinking about the same thing.

Dave broke the silence, "Think I'll take a walk, I will."

"Need a flashlight, Dave?"

He smiled, "No, don't think I will."

Steve nodded in understanding.

"I hope you find her, Dave."

He walked down the porch stairs, stopped to look at the pond one more time. Then he turned to look at Steve and winked.

"So do I, Stevie." Dave strolled around behind the store and disappeared from view.

Steve reached over to an old radio sitting on a small table behind the chair. He switched it on. It glowed, hummed for a minute, then settled in on the frequency to which it was tuned. An old song was playing.

It was *Moonlight Serenade*.

Made in the USA